Loved by a Gentleman

Alizee Kay

Grosvenor House
Publishing Limited

This book is published by
Grosvenor House Publishing Ltd
Link House
140 The Broadway, Tolworth, Surrey, KT6 7HT.
www.grosvenorhousepublishing.co.uk

This book is a work of fiction. Names, characters, places,
organisations and incidents are either products of the author's
imagination or used fictitiously. Any resemblance to actual events, places,
organisations or persons, living or dead, is entirely coincidental.

A CIP record for this book
is available from the British Library

ISBN 978-1-83975-832-4

ACKNOWLEDGMENTS

With particular thanks to my mother, Maria Bucsi, for her all-time support. With or without a national lockdown. And for making sure that us, her children, never felt alone.

Chapter 1

'Who is it?' asked Beatrice.

'Can I come in?'

With her heart pounding, Beatrice opened the door. Logan stood there leaning against the wall. There was something so irresistible about him when he did that. Something irresistible that captivated Beatrice and something magical that made her feel safe at the same time. Without him ever making a promise. All she ever wanted was to slide under his arm and kiss his neck above the collar of his shirt. She was never able to resist his charm.

Logan always wore the cleanest shirts under his suits. His suits cost a fortune, a fortune for Beatrice, in which he looked so incredibly dashing. He had a tall and slim figure, and he always had a tan. Beatrice never knew, to keep that all year round, how he was able to manage.

He shaved every day without fail, and he maintained a clean haircut. He was a tidy man. He was one in a thousand. His shirt, at the top, was never buttoned up. Beatrice wondered whether he could tell that she was staring at his neck during every conversation they ever had. And they had plenty of those; Logan was Beatrice's boss.

She never forgot her first appraisal with him; a well-respected man in a suit asking her to talk about herself for three hours. *My idea of a working day*, she thought.

Today, that exact same man was knocking on her door in the middle of the night. Beatrice wanted to run into his arms but instead, she just stood there, gazing at his neck.

Beatrice didn't own sexy lingerie yet, somehow, she was wearing some. She was wearing a black lace bralette with matching panties. Wearing matching underwear was also not frequently accomplished by Beatrice. On this night, however, she was standing at the door of a hotel room, in front of the man of her dreams, and she was sexy.

Logan took a long step forward. Long enough to reach Beatrice.

Beatrice always admired Logan's lips. And now, she was in his arms, wearing beautiful lingerie and kissing him, finally kissing him. The fireworks in her entire body gave her such a light weight, she didn't even realise how he managed to lift her up, take her into the room, and lie her gently onto the bed.

His lips moved further down her neck.

He stroked her waist, her thighs, and her legs. With every touch, he made her breath louder and louder. He gently pulled her panties down.

Beatrice wanted more.

She arched her back, with both arms holding onto the headboard. She moved up on the bed and opened her legs. She wanted to feel his weight on her. As he moved closer, she could feel her entire body shaking. She had waited years for this moment. And now it was finally happening.

With one hand in between her legs and the other grabbing onto one of her breasts, Beatrice woke up suddenly. She was at home in her bedroom wearing her pyjamas. She hadn't seen Logan for over a year, but in her dream, she could still feel the fireworks in her entire body. He always had the ability to make her feel that way. All he had to do was to look deep into her eyes and she was away.

Beatrice had green eyes. Or at least that's what she preferred to think. She had beautiful, seductive eyes, but she could never quite tell what colour they were. It depended on the colour of the clothes she wore. She had long, dark brown hair, and she was fit for her age. She was 35. Beatrice always knew where she ranked from one to ten. She liked to receive compliments. *Rewards for my efforts*, so she thought.

* * *

Beatrice always felt nervous driving through the narrow roads that surrounded her entire neighbourhood. She loved the scenic views, of course, but many a times she wished there were an easier way to get to and from her house. Other times, it gave her the thrills she needed.

The high demand of concentration while driving through the bends usually made her stay away from daydreaming.

Not today, so it seemed. All she could think about was Logan; how was it, that even after a year, he could still highjack her dream?

She fell in love with Logan after about two years of working with him and for the best part of six years after that, she was unable to escape this love. When their paths separated, Beatrice was prepared to move on too.

Now she was the catering manager in a beautiful country hotel that held luxurious corporate and private events. She was born to do this job. The high-profile clients and the pressure of delivering luxury so seamlessly were deemed worthy of her commitments. Her team trusted her ability to deliver above and beyond every time, while her attention to the finest details mesmerised her guests.

'Nita, hi! How are you?' Beatrice put her phone on speaker.

'I can't believe you're not coming in today, Beatrice! What if I can't deliver? I'm going to cause a disaster and we will be ridiculed. No one will ever want to hold an event here.'

Nita, short for Anita, was one of Beatrice's assistant managers. She always knew what to do in every situation, but she liked to make herself look less capable. Unknown to her, she was surprisingly good at troubleshooting and working under pressure. After over exaggerating every obstacle, telling you that there was no way for a job to be done, she went on to completing it with the lightest of ease. She was a great girl to have around if you knew how to handle her. Even though Beatrice was a master at working with her by now, she sometimes wished she had a more experienced assistant manager. Someone that needed less of her support, and someone who would just get on with it, she thought.

'You'll be absolutely fine, just like every other time,' said Beatrice. 'Now, go on, and make me proud like you always do!'

Beatrice was on her way to the annual conference where she was nominated for one of the awards. She had been nominated and awarded many a times before, yet every time she felt privileged and not at all entitled. To her, staying humble was an essential part of being great at what you did. And a familiar feeling.

She looked to her left onto the passenger seat. There laid a resume. On top of it, a note read "Call him!" in Beatrice's handwriting.

Chapter 2

'And the winner is... Beatrice Holt, from Autumn Leaves House Hotel!'

Beatrice was seated at the back of the room. No one could ever tell exactly how scared she was when she was placed in the middle of attention. She considered herself shy and someone who preferred to listen rather than talk at social gatherings, while other people hoped to hear her voice.

Her topics were always inspiring and filled with intelligence she got from thinking outside the box. Her peers enjoyed her presence, and her input to any team effort was unpredictable. She was often labelled as one who approached every situation from a completely different angle. She had a unique quality, and she had the ability to keep everyone interested to know about her every move.

She fascinated many.

Her overwhelming experience on stage, and the three-course meal that followed it, made Beatrice feel desperate for some fresh air. They never served more than three courses at these conferences as no one even bothered to get to dessert.

Everybody was too tipsy by then.

The seating plans were well designed to get people to socialise with those not in their immediate circle. You would think that after many years of trying, they'd realise that no matter what they do, people will always mingle from table to table. Place cards didn't matter much at these events.

The room was situated on the first floor of the venue with access to a beautiful balcony in the middle of the forest. Beatrice made her way outside. It was a late September night with a little bit of a breeze but not too cool to have to wear a jacket. The sky was clear.

Beatrice could see the moon from where she stood. It was a moon sickle, and to her, it was ever so near.

'Hi.'

Beatrice turned around and saw Logan standing behind her. Her heart stopped for a second but then she realised it was the perfect time for him to meet her. She was wearing a mid-length cocktail dress in a pencil shape. She always knew it was the best shape to complement her body. On top of that, her hair was flawlessly set on her shoulders while her skin looked radiant in the subtle lighting of the balcony.

'Hi,' she said quietly. 'How did you get here? I mean, what are you doing here? I thought this was a private event,' Beatrice asked as she looked around to see if he was followed by a security man.

'I've been in a meeting in this hotel all day and I knew you were coming here tonight. I wanted to see you.' Logan smiled.

Beatrice never knew how, but Logan was always able to go wherever he wanted to. Behind the scenes of events and VIP rooms, even. He had a way of talking himself in and out of situations as it pleased him.

He leaned forward to kiss Beatrice on her cheek, and he whispered kindly, 'Are you not happy to see me?'

'Of course I am. Hundreds of times I imagined bumping into you but never in my mind did it happen at such a perfect time,' answered Beatrice with a smile.

'I hear you won an award tonight. You must be thrilled.'

'I am,' said Beatrice humbly, 'I cannot tell you how happy I am to see you, however. Are you well?'

'Yes,' Logan replied. 'I'm told you like your new job.'

Beatrice had been in her current position for about a year now. She didn't consider it new anymore, but at that moment, it seemed as if they only parted yesterday. It was the hardest decision she ever made.

Working with Logan was dreamy. He was not only a decent employer, but he was also a decent human being. He had compassion. Beatrice repaid him with her loyalty until her love and devotion grew too difficult to bear, and she knew she had to leave him.

Logan looked more handsome than ever before. He wore Beatrice's favourite dark blue suit. A man in formal wear, she was never able to ignore. Today, she found it ever so hard to believe that Logan was standing in front of her eyes on the same day that she had a dream about him. *What a coincidence*! she thought. They must have both wanted to see each other so badly that the universe had no choice but to make it happen.

'You look wonderful tonight.'

'Thank you, I just needed a bit of fresh air,' Beatrice replied. She was blushing, unable to hide.

She was extremely nervous every time she met Logan. It always took her about twenty minutes before she got comfortable being in his presence. Or until he mercifully paid her a compliment.

He had the ability to positively intimidate her and wonderfully overpower her entire existence. When he was with her, to Beatrice, nothing else mattered.

'Shall we go for a walk?' Logan spoke again.

Beatrice placed her arm around his, wondering if she was still in her dream.

She decided to break the silence as they made their way towards the lake. 'Yes, so... I do love my job. My boss is just like you. A leader with compassion and we share similar values. I am incredibly pleased with the way things turned out,' she continued.

Logan smiled. He was focusing very much on the "just like you" part as if he were a little bit jealous of this other man who was now in charge of Beatrice. This other man, who was able to see her and talk to her any time he wanted to. Logan always knew he couldn't have her and until she stopped working with him, he never let anybody else have her either. The thought of her being with someone else, most probably the only thing out of his hands, was killing him. He was no longer able to influence what she was doing, where she was going, and with whom she was talking.

'Just like me?' he asked, almost flirting.

'No, not exactly like you,' Beatrice replied, feeling a little embarrassed.

Even after a year, every time she thought of Logan, her whole experience, and every conversation with him flew right back into her memory. The touch of his hands and the look in his eyes. With just one glance, into her body, he sent an army of butterflies. When he touched her, she couldn't feel her heart from shaking. It always happened as if it had happened by accident. Beatrice could never tell exactly whether he meant to do it, or if it was, in fact, inadvertent.

They sat down on a bench overlooking the lake. It was still, and peaceful, with only the sound of crickets chirping keeping everybody awake. They talked a little more about how they were doing at work and the usual small talk topics. Logan complimented Beatrice a hundred times. The way she looked at him, and the way she smiled. He always saw a great deal of admiration in her eyes.

'Come, I'll take you back to your room.'

He was desperate to make sure that if she couldn't spend it with him, Beatrice spent the night alone.

Chapter 3

Apart from the thrill of having to work under pressure with high profile clients, another thing Beatrice loved about her job was its location. Autumn Leaves House Hotel was situated in the middle of the British countryside in Buckinghamshire, not too far from where she lived.

The roads, leading to the beautiful building, and its surrounding estate, looked like pictures taken from a fairy tale. Beatrice couldn't believe how lucky she was to be able to drive into this wonderland every day. Once she got close enough to be able to take it all in, her mood already lifted.

She felt glorious, she felt enchanted.

The building had an established authority over the neighbouring sphere. It had been refurbished many a times before, but some of its unique features at the front, they decided to spare. Beatrice especially loved the original steps built into the driveway. She used to stand on top of them and admire the view. It was the perfect spot to daydream and the perfect spot to muse.

In front of her, the country's biggest water fountain laid in the middle of a well-groomed park. It was magnificent in daylight and truly magical in the dark. All around it, further in the distance, evergreens grew thick over the years.

Beatrice was greeted with a huge round of applause as she stepped inside the hotel. 'Thank you, all, I could not do this job without your hard work and commitment. This round of applause, as far as I'm concerned, is just as much for you. So, hear hear, and cheers to all of you.'

'Hurray!' cheered everyone.

Nita placed a glass of champagne into Beatrice's hand. 'And here's to another successful year!' Beatrice said.

Walking away from the crowd, Nita grabbed the opportunity to brief Beatrice on the event, which, surprisingly to herself only, she handled exceptionally well. Beatrice already made the directors aware of how successful it all had been. And, as far as she was concerned, to worry about it so much, there was no need.

Nita was a girl considered beautiful by many. They looked remarkably similar, and she was only a couple of years younger than Beatrice. A big difference, however, was the strengths in their features. While Beatrice was softer and gentler, Nita was more abrupt and borderline monstrous. She had a contagious smile, however, that had the ability to make her indelicate first impressions disappear within seconds. She liked to dress loudly, and she wasn't afraid of bright colours. She wore red lipstick. Beatrice didn't mind it. She believed it made her smile more visible and even from afar she was able to look incredible.

'Excellent work, Nita, as always. Well done!' said Beatrice, ready to move away from the conversation.

'Oh, and... Um... Arian is already here,' Nita added quickly.

'Arian? Who is Arian?'

'Your candidate. He sent his resume in for our part-time team member positions, and he told me you asked him to come in for an interview.' Nita was a little suspicious about it all, as she was the one usually in charge of recruiting team members.

'Well, where is he?' asked Beatrice as she turned around.

She saw a slim, young man with dark hair greeting people in a crowd. His body language was open and welcoming, his voice ever so polite. He had a kind look in his eyes. He was incredibly charming. He drew everybody's attention around him. Beatrice knew she had never seen this man in the hotel before. He didn't work there. Of that, she couldn't be surer.

'Hi, my name is Beatrice, and you are?' she asked, holding out for a handshake.

'Good morning, miss, I'm Arian, glad to meet you! It looks beautiful around here.'

Arian was wearing a pair of jeans that were either new or very well looked after. He wore them with a checked shirt that looked like it was meant to be worn around the family ranch in the middle of Texas. Beatrice wasn't too keen on the shirt, but she decided to make her peace with it. After all, it wasn't inappropriate if you were a team member candidate.

'Shall we sit down?' she asked, pointing towards one of the coffee tables in the lobby. 'Can I get you a drink?'

'I will take a cup of coffee, if I may,' said Arian politely.

Beatrice looked at one of her team members without saying a word. An americano and a large bottle of mineral water were already on the table by the time they finished their polite chit-chat about the weather.

Beatrice had a fantastic team. People had respect for her and time after time, they decided to stay with her. In her colleagues, she considered loyalty the most desirable quality. She trained her team well, and she treated them even better. In a short period of time, she was able to make everyone see what a good job looked like, and once a team was built, they stuck around.

Beatrice sat there watching Arian, almost not even listening to what he was saying. She was more interested in the way he was sitting and the way he was holding his cup of coffee. He was looking around curiously, checking the cleanliness of the tables, the chairs, the pictures, and everything else. One of the paintings on the wall wasn't straight, he pointed out. Beatrice was extremely pleased with his observations and how much he cared about the details. 'A man with high standards! I love him!' she said out loud.

Her mind about giving Arian a manager position was already made up. Arian came from a fine dining background, which Beatrice knew would complement her team perfectly well. What she was experiencing right now, she believed to be a miracle. She was mesmerised by his aurora from the minute she laid eyes on him. She knew that in this dashing young man she had found the assistant manager of her dreams. That's how impressed she was by him. The interview went well from then on. They made each other laugh and they paid each other compliments. If it were a first date, it would have been remarkable.

'And now, my last question, Arian...'

'You said that already,' he interrupted teasing.

Beatrice admired confidence in men. She was always considered somewhat distant to many of them. It took only the very brave to dare to ask her out. Arian was cheeky, confident, incredibly smart, and a true gentleman. Beatrice didn't mind his teasing and she made sure he knew this by giving him a smile. Courage, after all, was a virtue and not a sin in Beatrice's mind.

She said goodbye to him at the entrance overlooking the estate. Arian shook her hand and thanked her for meeting with him before he walked away. 'It was good to see you and thank you for your time.'

'Like him?' asked Nita, who suddenly appeared.

'Like him? I wish-he-wasn't-married like him,' Beatrice replied.

Chapter 4

With its subtle furnishings, the drawing room's original purpose was almost redefined. During the day, the masters of the house used to retreat to it when they wanted a more private moment, and after dinner, it was where the ladies withdrew while they waited for the gentlemen to finish their cigars. It had an unusual feel to it that even Beatrice was never able to describe. She felt at home in that room, and it was where she liked to spend most of her time. It was a cold room, however, and even with its renaissance windows on two of its walls, it didn't see much sunlight. Almost ever.

Today, it was hardly ever used by any of the guests, and when it was, it was only available upon prior request. Beatrice always knew when she could hold her meetings there. It was a decent size, with some of its original features still intact. In Beatrice's mind, it was comfortable, it was elegant, it was perfect.

'Good morning, good to see you,' said Arian as he entered the room. He was talking to everyone, but he was only looking at Beatrice. She was seated the furthest away, and it was obvious to all how eager he was to get close to her. Beatrice could only hope that her excitement, on the other hand, was slightly less transparent. As she sat on the sofa, watching him approach, she felt her heart beat faster and faster. Her entire body was on fire by the time she could feel his arms around her.

In the past two weeks, Arian turned out to be worthy of his position. He was cheerful, and he had the ability to talk to anyone from any kind of background. He had a unique sense of humour and he was always able to make Beatrice laugh. He was kind, and he was considerate. He was supportive, and he made it clear to Beatrice that he was there to help her with whatever challenges she had. He proved himself to be reliable and a true gentleman.

Arian sat down on the couch next to Beatrice. He enjoyed participating in her meetings. His input was valuable and relevant. In fact, no one was ever able to tell he was one of the newest managers. He had the knowledge, and he had the skills. He was eager too. Beatrice found everything she had ever dreamed of in this remarkable young man that she soon started to call The Talented Mr Arian.

'Everyone, thank you all for coming. I know I don't need to tell you all, the Devire event will be one of our biggest ever. We cannot afford any mistakes,' Beatrice stressed.

'I'm in,' Arian said with firmness.

He had a unique way to assure people, with his mannerism, that he wanted only the best for the guests, for the team and, not to mention, for Beatrice. He showed her unconditional respect. There was not a task in the world he wouldn't do for her. If it helped her, he was its fan. While her other managers relied on her feedback and observation, in only a matter of hours spent in the hotel, Arian was able to spot exactly the type of support she was in need of. For Beatrice it felt like she was working with a peer. A peer, who had the ability to reignite her deepest passions and make all her fears disappear.

Beatrice quickly wrapped up the meeting. As everyone was leaving the room, she asked Arian if he could stay behind. Arian loved his private moments with her, and he never had to be asked twice.

They both started tidying the tables and chairs after everyone had left. Arian always made sure the cushions on the armchairs were plumped up and neatly kept. The rest of the team didn't know the difference.

'Tonight is going to be a big one, are you sure you're going to be able to handle it?' asked Beatrice.

'Leave it with me! I'm sure there are things I don't know one hundred per cent, but I can't think of anything I couldn't handle myself.'

Beatrice loved the fact that Arian, as confident as he might have been, was not afraid to admit when he didn't know something. He asked questions and he asked to be shown again, and again. As many times as it was needed. If there was one thing he wasn't, it was a quick learner. In Beatrice's mind, however, he was only taking his time to consume the information and already work out ways in which he could help improve them.

'You know something, Beatrice?' asked Arian rhetorically. 'My life will never be the same again. Even my wife has commented on how much I've changed since I met you.'

'Yes... Uhm... Yes... Uhm...' Beatrice wasn't sure how to respond to that.

For the last two weeks, every minute of every day, Beatrice and Arian spent together. They wanted to find out everything about each other. Professional conversations turned to personal only after a few minutes. They followed each other everywhere. With an undeniable energy between them, they were soulmates and kindred spirits with the greatest possibility for the most passionate love affair.

After making sure the room was left in an immaculate condition, they both stopped for a second, feeling satisfied. Beatrice was about to turn away from him when Arian, with both of his hands, suddenly grabbed her by the waist on each side. She could feel his strength trying to hold her close, and it made her feel excited. As he gave her a hug, she felt her entire body electrocuted. The sensation was so strong that she could feel her legs shaking.

He leaned in, and he gave her a gentle kiss on her cheek.

Beatrice always knew he was perfectly capable, with his intellect, of capturing her mind, but she only just realised how easily he was also able to fulfil her sexual appetite. They had chemistry. Her heart was thinking it, her body was feeling it, it was only her brain rejecting it.

Chapter 5

Beatrice was walking up and down her office, feeling nervous and uncomfortable. She knew she had to talk to Arian. These feelings she was having, she had to stop them happening. *I'm evil and vile.* Cruelly and unmercifully judging herself, with her face in her hands, she collapsed on her desk.

It's happened to her again, except this time she wasn't on the receiving end. She couldn't help but remember the time she felt her endless love for her previous employer, Logan Townsend. When he looked into her eyes, she could feel butterflies. The feel of his hand gave her body a sensation that made her smile for an entire week. The constant conjecturing, however, whether he could feel the same, used to absorb her every day. It was like torture; it was like pain. When they separated, she was finally free and sane she could remain.

Now, she had Arian in her life.

He stood close to her, and he touched her. He made her want him. Beatrice was right back where she began. It was just too painful, and too hard to reject. Somehow, she had to build a wall, and put an end to it, once and for all.

'Come in! I'm sure you know the reason why I asked you here.'

'To tell you the truth, no, I don't know,' said Arian. He did know, he didn't think Beatrice would be bold enough to bring it up in a conversation though.

'Arian, I've been watching your behaviour recently. As you know, I'm incredibly pleased with your work here and that includes your ability to influence your team,' said Beatrice confidently. 'I would like to ask you, however, that you keep a distance when you are talking to me. I don't want you to touch my hand or any part of my body, in fact. There is no harm done, I just cannot live my life wondering whether you meant to touch me or if it was just an accident,' said Beatrice, now with a little less confidence.

'But I don't understand, I thought you liked it.'

'It doesn't matter, Arian; you have to stop,' Beatrice said.

Arian pretended to be offended a little, but very politely he told Beatrice he understood where she was coming from. Beatrice had great empathy for the feelings of her team and people in general. Right now, she wasn't sure whether she acted properly, however. She didn't mean to hurt Arian's feelings and he was cruel enough not to hide the fact that she might have done exactly that.

When Beatrice was about to leave the room, Arian kindly asked her to stay behind. 'Yes, Arian?' she asked, bona fide.

He stepped closer to her. Close enough to touch her.

Beatrice couldn't think about anything else other than how much she wanted her entire body to feel his hands. Being so close to him had such an effect on her. She had to physically fight the temptation that came over her.

Arian knew exactly how he made her feel, and now he was punishing her for telling him not to go near. 'Do me a favour, Beatrice, stop thinking about it so much and enjoy it,' he whispered gently into her ear.

Chapter 6

Beatrice lived in a small cottage in the beautiful county of Buckinghamshire in rural England. She had a cosy home with natural wood flooring and original beams in her low ceiling. Her open-plan kitchen and living room was of a smaller size but she gave the area a special character with the way she arranged her furnishings. Beatrice didn't take a lot of time out of work but when she did, she enjoyed being at home. Most of all, she loved sitting at her dining table reading the newspaper.

She heard her phone beep. *It's got to be Arian*, she thought, keen to believe.

'I hope you're having a splendid time.'

Beatrice found Arian's choice of words delightful and intimidating at the same time. Sometimes she almost felt like she wasn't worthy of his conversations. She admired how collected he always was. Most of the time, she felt she should be the one working for him and not the other way round. In her opinion, such exquisite mannerism only existed within royalty and the people alike.

Beatrice didn't keep an awfully close relationship with her managers outside of work. None of her colleagues ever visited her home, and no one called or texted her on her days off. Except when they needed her help with something, and except Arian. Arian would message to see how she was almost every day. He would call her, and if she didn't pick up, he would leave her a message on her voicemail.

'My mobile providers will start to think I have finally got a boyfriend,' said Beatrice smiling.

On her phone records, Arian's number had the most reoccurring appearances. His calls were not only frequent, but they also lasted hours and hours. No matter where they were, if they were not at work, with less possibility for interruptions, they could talk about anything and everything almost.

'How come you're not engaged to be married yet?' he asked out of the blue.

'I'm too special, I only get to appear in the sequel,' Beatrice said.

She preferred to believe that she was too fabulous for ordinary men to ask her out, until they found their true purpose in the world and became worthy of her magnificence. The idea that she was simply not wanted by men was just too depressing a thought for her to bear.

'I think you are amazing; you are the most beautiful woman I ever met. When men look at you, they think how much they want to get naked with you,' said Arian feeling embarrassed. Beatrice didn't know if this was a compliment, or if she should feel offended, but she didn't have much more time to further consider it before he continued. 'That's because they don't know you. They don't know that behind this beautiful and incredibly sexy body there's an intelligent mind and a kind heart.

Wow, a compliment, definitely a compliment, said Beatrice to herself with relief. No one had ever said anything like that to her before, and even though he said it over the phone, Beatrice could feel Arian's affections towards her undeniably.

'Hm... Favourite superhero?' she asked, trying to change the subject quickly.

'Batman,' replied Arian without hesitation.

'Great answer,' said Beatrice. 'Powerful, mysterious and handsome. Favourite Disney character?' she continued. 'I wonder what you would have thought of me if I had asked you these questions in your interview?'

'I would have thought, *finally! A lady I can relate to.*'

* * *

Mondays used to be the quietest day in the hotel. After her managers' meetings, Beatrice would stick around for a while in order to catch up with some of her work around personnel. It was the perfect time for her to send out her weekly memos, envision the current week, and make a plan.

Arian was always there.

Every week, without fail, he used to order dinner for two, neatly organise a table in an empty conference room, and invite Beatrice to join him away from the rest of the team.

There were several conference rooms in the hotel with different shapes and sizes. The smallest one of them all was more like a private dining room with a single table in the middle, which didn't fit more than twelve people around it. It was almost too small for the size of the room, but that was precisely what made the dining experience more intimate, harmonious, and cosy. Everybody was able to hear everybody. As long as it wasn't used by any of the guests, Arian would choose that room to place their dinner sets. Out of all the rooms in the hotel, it was the most romantic, he could tell.

'Arian, you always make me feel like I should have changed into something more appropriate for these dinners,' said Beatrice, looking down on her outfit, dissatisfied.

'You look nice,' Arian replied. 'It's not like I'm in my white tie, but maybe next time,' he continued, as he held out for Beatrice's hand.

When they reached the table, Arian pulled out her chair, waited for her to sit down and placed her napkin on her lap before he sat down himself.

'Sometimes I feel like I'm in a different world when I'm with you,' Beatrice confessed.

The two of them set next to each other with a burning candle in the middle. They were halfway through their dinners when they realised they were not alone. Some of the crew members were watching them from the entrance of the room.

'I think they're whispering about us,' said Beatrice with a sudden sense of self-consciousness.

'Heavens! Is that a nuisance?' Arian asked, feeling a little bit nervous.

Every time he was about to find out what Beatrice thought about something he did or something he said, he got somewhat anxious. It was obvious to everyone but him, how fascinated Beatrice was about his qualities. She had to repeat a compliment several times before he was finally able to fully accept it. To Beatrice, it felt like he put himself under too much pressure. As if, in his mind, he could never be good enough to impress her.

'It is a little bit. I don't like to be the topic of conversations here.'

'I understand, I can't help how much I admire you though, I enjoy spending time with you,' replied Arian.

'I really like you too,' Beatrice said.

As they looked deep into each other's eyes, Beatrice felt a tiny electric shock inside her body and she knew from that moment she was right.

It was love at first sight.

Chapter 7

'Come in,' said Marilena with the greatest compassion in her voice.

Beatrice walked through a beautifully hand-crafted front door, double the size of her own. Marilena lived in a big house full of space and full of light. Every time she went there, Beatrice felt mesmerised. To be able to see what looked good, and where, came naturally to Marilena, to be fair. Every piece of furniture, every ornament, curtain, and rug matched her style with excellence. Each of her rooms looked like they were uniquely designed with her own flair and finesse. They screamed class, elegance, luxury, and lavishness.

'You should be an interior designer,' Beatrice would say to her every day without fail. Not today. Today, she walked straight into the living room feeling gloomy and grey.

'Fuck it! Who cares if he's married?' asked Marilena rhetorically.

Marilena was Beatrice's best friend, and she was, in Beatrice's opinion, a little bit on the crazy side. They met about a year previously and from the moment they said hello, they both knew their feelings for each other would coincide.

Marilena was mad about fashion. She didn't have a mannequin figure, but she knew exactly what suited her and how to make herself look out of this world. She liked labels, and she had the money to pay for them. Beatrice could never click with girls who were too much into their looks, but somehow, she knew from the first instance that Marilena was different. What made her stand out from the crowd was her personality. She was just as down to earth as Beatrice. Honesty mattered more than anything to both of them. Apart from that, they couldn't have been any more different.

Marilena always said what she felt, the moment she felt it. She didn't hold back her feelings and she didn't mind who she offended. She was helping people grow into a better person in her own special way. Or that was what she liked to believe, in any case. 'You have two options. Option number one; exit number one. Option number two; exit number two,' she would say to anyone not delivering up to her standards.

Marilena used to be one of Beatrice's assistant managers until she was promoted. Now, she was Beatrice's peer. Beatrice loved the fact that she could finally talk to her more like a friend, since she was no longer holding her development gear. Now they could tell each other everything.

Beatrice called her Miss Marilena because of her classy and elegant personality. She would have called her a lady if it weren't for her dirty mind, and her mouth, which Beatrice thought was even more filthy.

'What do you mean, who cares? I care a great deal. Every time I'm with this guy, all I can think about is how much I want to kiss him.'

'And does he feel the same?'

'Well, that's why I'm here. I need your opinion. How can someone be so affectionate, flirtatious, kind and everything else that matters in love and relationships? He must feel the same way. It's like I can feel his love for me.'

In her previous relationships, men used to tell her how much they loved her, but Beatrice never felt it. With Arian it was different. He never told her he loved her, but she could feel it whenever she was in his presence. She felt his everlasting love put into everything he ever did for her. When he made her a cup of coffee, she could feel it was made with love. When he tried to comfort her in a stressful situation, she could feel his love and devotion. And when he touched her, beside the most amazing chemistry between them, she felt his love for her.

'All I can tell you, Beatrice, is that men will tell you compliments when they want to flirt with you but they don't spend hours on the phone if they want nothing from you.'

This made Beatrice feel reassured but she didn't know what to do next, however.

'I'll tell you what to do,' said Marilena. 'You need to ask him out. You need to spend a night together and see what happens. He has a lot to lose, and he will not make the first step. You have to be the one brave enough to do that.'

'You know I'm not like that, Marilena. If I were, I would have made a move with Logan years ago,' replied Beatrice.

Marilena knew of Logan but she never met him. She would listen to Beatrice's countless stories about this amazing man she loved so much but never dared touch. 'Don't be so unselfish again, Beatrice, you'll never be happy. You need to tell this man how you feel,' said Marilena abruptly. 'Listen, you are coming to Ibiza for my hen party, right?' she asked, jumping away from the subject.

When Beatrice and Marilena first met, Marilena was annoyed with Beatrice's constant dreaming of a beautiful wedding. She couldn't care less about finding the one or getting married. She was a confident young woman who had everything going for her and marriage was the last thing on her mind with a power to amuse her. Until about seven months ago, when she met Oliver. She fell head over heels, and she was now organising her wedding with a date set in the upcoming summer.

Beatrice still didn't believe it had happened to her best friend, who didn't even care about love and romance. It was like they swapped places. Beatrice had lost all her faith in marriage, and Marilena couldn't talk about anything else but her wedding planning.

'Of course I will.' said Beatrice. She didn't feel like going to Ibiza, but Marilena was her best friend, and, for the world, she knew she wouldn't want to miss it. She stayed for two more hours talking about the ring, the dress, the cake, and everything else to do with Marilena's big fat wedding. 'I'd better get going,' she said after a while.

'Do me a favour, Beatrice, book a room in your fabulous hotel this week, and take Arian with you,' said Marilena at the door as she kissed her goodbye.

Beatrice couldn't think about anything else on her drive home. She wished she had the courage to take Arian into one of the rooms. She imagined him holding her hand as they were walking up the stairs. Arian in a suit and her, in the most beautiful evening dress. With her eyes locked into his, she didn't even look where they were going. Once in the room, he stroked her face with his hand slowly moving further down her neck, her breast, and her waist. Feeling nervous and excited at the same time, Beatrice watched him take his jacket off without haste. She stood there silently, waiting for him to touch her again. He stepped closer. Close enough to reach her lips with his. He kissed her with so much intensity she could no longer keep her hands off him. She slid her fingers through his hair, pulling his head closer to her body. She wanted to feel his hands on her. On her back, on her breast, on her waist and inside her legs. He unzipped her dress, letting it fall onto the floor. While keeping his eyes on her, he laid her gently onto the bed. With her entire body shaking, she watched him undress. He moved on top of her, kissing her thighs, waist, and breast. Beatrice breathed out loud and arched her back. With her eyes closed, grabbing onto the bedsheet with both her hands, she opened her legs. She wanted him to kiss her there.

Beeeeep! Beatrice opened her eyes.

'Fuck! I do need to get laid,' she said out loud.

Chapter 8

'Take me to heaven!' said Beatrice as she sat inside Arian's car. They were on their way to pick up some Christmas decorations. The hotel usually organised the main rooms and the hallways but inside the drawing room, Beatrice liked to make a special effort. Every year she did it all by herself, but she was not going to say no when Arian offered to help. She had fabulous taste but every time she was placed before a decision on what to spend her money on, she preferred to get a second opinion. Arian understood quality. Beatrice knew this from the moment they met. If there were anyone she would allow to help her decide on something as important as Christmas decorations, it had to be Arian.

'Oh my God, Arian! How have I never been to this place before? Look at all these decorations! I'm in Christmas heaven. You really did take me there,' said Beatrice, smiling.

Arian smiled back at her, slightly embarrassed. They had a mutual, unspoken understanding since the moment they met. Comments like that had two different meanings and they brought this incredible intimacy between them. It was like they could tell each other everything. Beatrice had never felt so comfortable with anyone else before. She was ready to be taken by this remarkably gentle man, whose love for her she could feel more and more.

Arian took Beatrice onto the top floor where all the decorations and trees were kept. Standing on the escalators, moving up slowly, Beatrice was still admiring this magical world she felt she was in. Once they got to the top of the stairs, Arian walked her around looking at everything that sparkled and everything that glared. Holding her hand, only for a little bit, but yes, holding her hand, he walked her up and down the lanes of bauble heaven. Who felt happier by this magic, Beatrice couldn't tell. She kept wondering whether it would be just as magical if she came on her own, or whether she would feel the same way if Nita was her chaperon.

Every year at work or in her private life, Beatrice had to do her Christmas shopping by herself, together with everything else. When she bought furniture from IKEA, she had to build it herself. When she wanted pictures on her walls, she had to hang them by herself. She didn't especially like shopping, but today, today she couldn't imagine herself enjoying anything better than that particular minute.

'Cool white,' said Arian.

'Are you sure? Everything is warm in the room, even the spotlights in the ceiling. The rest of the decorations are gold. I don't think that these are the ones that we should go for.'

'Trust me!' replied Arian.

Beatrice had a weakness. She was rather stubborn, but with her elegance and class, she always managed to convince public opinion. Not this time. Arian was so certain of his ideas, Beatrice couldn't help but approve the cool white fairy lights.

Arian placed the decorations in his boot without letting Beatrice lift anything that he considered to be a little bit on the heavy side. Beatrice was not used to such a treatment.

'After you!' said Arian as he locked the boot.

'Where are you taking me?' asked Beatrice.

Behind the store, covered in white and filled with loved up couples, was the town's ice rink.

This has got to be the cheesiest moment of my life, thought Beatrice. 'Arian, stop! I cannot be ice skating with you in December. This only happens in movies,' said Beatrice, fearing what was about to happen to be the most romantic moment of her life. Arian's confidence swept her away entirely. The next thing she knew, they were in each other's arms, skating to Mariah Carey.

On the ride back to the hotel, neither of them said a word. Arian kept his eyes on the road, and on Arian, Beatrice kept hers. They didn't need any words for them to know what they were thinking. To Beatrice, it felt unreal. It felt like magic. Even when they weren't in the same room together, they could finish each other's sentences.

'You know what I think, Arian? These cool white lights actually give definition to the tree at the back. They somehow emphasise its presence. You are amazing!' Beatrice said. They had spent the rest of the afternoon decorating the room, drinking hot chocolate and sharing childhood memories. It was the perfect day for Beatrice. Arian didn't answer. He just stood there, looking at her, smiling.

* * *

'Please accept my deepest apologies for my being late.' On the phone Arian was even more polite. He was on his way to Beatrice's end-of-year meeting. It was not compulsory to attend. It was usually held on weekdays when Arian had to care for his children, and Beatrice couldn't reasonably expect him to drop his family commitments. Arian, being a newbie and very eager to be part of the bigger picture, insisted. With the condition that he was able to bring little George with him. Beatrice had no objections. Deep down, she was very eager to meet this young boy who was, in her opinion, the luckiest person. He was forced to spend all of his time with Arian, after all. Beatrice was sure, when they were together, every minute was filled with plenty of charming-the-ladies, plenty of fun, and plenty of laughter.

'Please don't worry. Absolutely no rush. Is George with you?'

'Yes, he's the reason we're running late. He's been a little terror this morning, probably testing how much I can tolerate.'

The meeting had already finished by the time Arian and little George arrived. They sat down quietly on the couch. Beatrice, sitting next to them, was admiring the way Arian was looking at his boy. She was able to tell straight away how good a father he was. And as much as Arian wanted to impress others, Beatrice noticed just how much the others wanted him to be impressed by their manners. It was like they were looking for his blessings and compliments. Even his little boy looked back at him with the admiration of the greatest. Beatrice used to tell him he should be a president.

Beatrice felt compelled to keep them entertained. Especially little George. She was unsure of baby etiquette, however, and she felt embarrassed by not knowing what to say to him. Arian let him go wobbling around. Beatrice got scared every time he fell on his bottom while Arian didn't seem to mind. He had this idea that children needed to learn by falling. He talked to his boy as if he were an adult. To him, baby talk was boring.

Beatrice imagined Arian to be a great father from the moment they met. The truth in it, with her own eyes, she was finally able to witness. George was dressed well and crisply clean. Of course, at this age, boys didn't get into much trouble yet. Mud was kept outside the world of prams.

Beatrice decided to stay with the charming two for just a little while, but when Arian asked for a cup of coffee, she realised she wasn't going to do any more work. Coffee with Arian meant long conversations. And so it was. They talked a lot about him, and his adorable son the most. 'He will be a football player and I will be his agent,' said Arian, making Beatrice smile.

Arian was able to tell the most ridiculous ideas with the greatest of seriousness. Beatrice knew he was joking, yet she imagined a handsome football player being walked around the press by his father. To get him on the air after a winning match. Beatrice's mind was that picturesque. When she heard something, she imagined it. When she imagined it, it showed all over her face. Arian loved talking to her. She blushed every time he paid her a compliment. Her blushing gave him the greatest satisfaction. It was like he was able to win her heart over and over again.

'What is he singing?' asked Beatrice, watching George standing by the window.

'It's a nursery rhyme he learnt recently.'

'I can hear the melody. It's very pretty. Something with a bird?' she asked, not fully understanding the words.

George ran back to his father quickly. Arian picked him up and let him sit on his lap. 'With the ladies, he's like a magnet.'

'I know, I can feel it. I am one of them,' Beatrice said without taking her eyes off them.

Chapter 9

It was a stunning December. Snow was falling almost every day. Even though it never stayed exceptionally long, it made looking out the hotel windows feel even more magical this time of the year. The fountain had been turned off by now. The evergreens in the distance had a hint of snow over them. Beatrice used to spend her evenings by the window admiring the snowflakes even if they could only ever be seen falling under the lamp-posts along the driveway.

Large, corporate parties arrived almost every day. Hundreds of companies booked their Christmas celebrations at the hotel. Many of them return guests, remembering Beatrice and her team from the previous year. Beatrice finally believed she was in the right place at the right time. After a busy Christmas period she liked to thank her team for their hard work and the perfect way to do that was to invite everybody to stay behind for a little get-together after a big event.

As she walked into the lobby, she saw Arian among a group of people she cared nothing about. When he spotted her, he couldn't take his eyes of her. From then on, he was drawn to her like a magnet. They spent the entire evening either standing next to each other or starring at each other from a distance. There was an undeniable energy between them, which they gave up fighting against from the first instance.

When Beatrice finished her speech, everybody toasted to a successful year and exchanged their Christmas gifts. For the rest of the evening, Beatrice and Arian enjoyed sitting side by side with their knees touching occasionally. With every touch a little spark ran through Beatrice's entire body. She didn't want the night to end. Soon, however, everybody started to organise themselves and leave the building. After they all disappeared, Beatrice noticed that Arian never left.

'I want to help you tidy up,' he said.

'Do you like your present?' asked Beatrice.

'It's perfect, absolutely perfect.'

"I wasn't looking for you, but it was when I found you, that I stopped looking", read Arian's card in Beatrice's handwriting.

'You know, Beatrice, this has two meanings,' he said with confidence.

'Yes, it has,' said Beatrice smiling, and slightly embarrassed.

Arian smiled back at her. He never understood why she was single. He thought she was intelligent, funny, beautiful, and sexy. She was everything he could ever admire in a lady. 'Tell me, Beatrice, what is it that you like in a man?'

'Ambition, confidence...'

'Confidence? Hmm... I'm going to have to work on that.' Beatrice found it hard to believe how different Arian saw himself from the way he was seen by others. He came across courageous and assertive. 'So, what are you doing tomorrow? he asked.

'I'm going to the centre for some last-minute shopping.'

'Great! I'll be in the centre myself. Let's meet at 10am. I'm not taking no for an answer.'

Through the back door, Beatrice walked Arian out. 'Good night, my darling Beatrice, and sweet dreams.'

Not surprisingly to herself, Beatrice dreamed of Arian that night.

* * *

Beatrice was standing in the middle of a beautifully decorated shopping centre on the morning of Christmas Eve, trying to remember the last time in December when she had time for a cup of coffee. The crowds cramming the passages between the shops, and the queues at the bottom of the escalators, added an extra feeling of rush to her already stressful last-minute shopping.

Looking around the delightfully decorated mall, however, gave Beatrice an instant feeling of serenity. The shop windows were decorated with shiny tinsels and gigantic baubles were hanging from the ceiling. By

Santa's grotto, an even more magical atmosphere was set by the fake snow and Christmas music blaring.

Not knowing which direction Arian would come from, Beatrice was looking around enthusiastically. His confidence in his decision-making and his secrecy around where he was, made Beatrice feel even more excited, and eager to see him. It all felt unreal to her, until her eyes caught up with him. He came rushing towards her, gave her a big hug and with the same rushing movement he started to lead the way. He was at home in the shopping centre and around every store. He knew exactly where he was going, and where he was taking her. Of that, he couldn't be surer.

'Can I ask you to bring me back here after? I wanted to pop into The Body Shop and I'm sure I would get lost without your help, which today I do not have the time for.'

'Of course I will,' replied Arian, 'I should be delighted. What would you like? Latte, and?' asked Arian. 'These doughnuts are amazing; you must try them.'

Arian was overly confident. He paid for everything before Beatrice could even think twice. He managed to bring her back to the days when girls paying for things was not even an option. Beatrice lived a free life. If she wanted to pay for something, she did. She had no desire for the man to pay for her drinks or dinners, not that she went to many of those, but when she did, she liked an equal sharing of the bill. Some days, she would invite a friend out, and on other days, she would let herself to be invited out. Arian's behaviour left her mesmerised. She felt it wasn't just him trying to be polite. She felt he was strong in his own wants and needs, knowledgeable in his manners and etiquette, and most of all, she felt he was in love. In love with Beatrice herself.

* * *

'See? Gentlemen do still exist!' replied Marilena.

Beatrice spent the rest of the day on the phone to Marilena, trying to describe her last few weeks at the hotel. She just couldn't believe it was all happening to her. All her life she waited for her Prince Charming, who never arrived. She, of course, had her times with men when she thought being cool and laid back was acceptable. That was when she was in her early twenties, however. But, for the best part of the last ten years, she admired gentlemen who knew how to treat a lady. And apart from Logan, she didn't seem to cross paths with many. And even Logan wasn't so gentle when he decided to reject her coldheartedly. For Beatrice, gentlemen were dead. Full stop. That was what made it ever so confusing when she was spending her time with Arian.

'The shocker of my life,' she said. 'It cannot be true.'

'Can't you just believe it, for once, that somebody actually likes you?'

'I guess,' said Beatrice.

49

But it wasn't just that they had similar likes, they also shared many identical dislikes. Beatrice found it even harder to believe that. *He's a spy, and he's planning my kidnapping,* she decided to think instead.

Chapter 10

Christmas Day was perfect for Beatrice. Everyone sat around the tree, watching the children play. The smell, the noise, and the everlasting laughter gave Beatrice a true feeling of love and gaiety. Frances, Beatrice's sister-in-law, was a doctor. She had only just finished her degree and was now working in a hospital in London. They couldn't see each other as many times as they wished during the year, working long hours for Beatrice and for Frances was more often than not foreseen. Being able to spend Christmas together was something they all held dear.

Beatrice liked to entertain at home. It was not often that she had people around, but when she did, she liked to make a special effort. Her tree was beautifully decorated and almost taller than her ceiling. She always liked the idea of a big tree. It brought back her childhood memories. They dressed her table elegantly, lit the fireplace, and after dinner they enjoyed the evening around the tree in peace and harmony. With her brother falling asleep on the floor, of course. And blaming it on Beatrice. 'It's your fault, and your fabulous meal,' he would say to her every year, without fail.

* * *

It was New Year's Eve. The night everybody was waiting for. The hotel held a gala dinner every year, and this year it was more glamorous than ever before. High-profile clients and regulars of the hotel were invited to celebrate in luxury and splendour.

Beatrice never did mind working on New Year's Eve at any of her jobs. She felt the atmosphere was cheerful, and it never actually felt like work. The parties always turned out to be great. This year they decided on a royal theme. The entire ballroom was filled with people dressed as emperors and empresses from around the world. The richest, and the most plentiful. All of them were introduced by their names and their titles, one after the other, as they entered the room.

Arian had the day off. He always had a hard time adjusting to part-time hours. He showed more commitment than most full-timers, and he felt left out every time he was not on the schedule when a special event was going on.

Beatrice knew that this time, however, it wasn't about being left out of work. It was the last day of the year and to each other, they just had to be near. It was no surprise to her at all when Arian drove into work to say Happy New Year. She was still upstairs and, by the time she was ready to make her way down, Arian was about to leave. He didn't have a lot of time to spare, but he was desperate to see her, it was his only reason for being there.

Beatrice's dress was made of white satin silk with beautiful open shoulders and golden appliqués. It had a ball gown shape with a perfectly fitted waistline, making her look like an actual princess, needless to say. She got the idea from the dress Romy Schneider wore for her Viennese Waltz with Franz Joseph, the Emperor of Austria, in the movie, *Sissi*. As she walked towards the crowd, she felt excitement and merriment. The entire room was filled with glee.

'You look wonderful tonight, absolutely amazing,' said Arian. He had little George with him. The large crowd and the music blaring made him feel agitated and frightened. Hiding behind his father's legs, he watched the crew handing out glasses of champagne to every guest.

Arian decided to take him outside when he began to cry. Beatrice walked out with them. It was the most beautiful evening in a while. There was a tiny bit of snow, making the view even more magnificent. They stopped on top of the steps for a second to be able to take it all in. Beatrice felt like a princess in a fairy tale, standing in front of her very own palace. As they made their way towards the gardens, Arian let little George run ahead. 'Any big plans for the new year?' he asked.

'No, not yet,' Beatrice said. 'How about you?' she asked Arian.

'I don't know, sometimes I wonder what it would be like if I had chosen a different path. Sometimes I wish to be free again.'

Beatrice was wondering whether she should get him to talk some more, but instead, she just stood there without saying anything at all. She could feel his sadness. When she heard little George playing in the distance, she decided to take a step forward. 'But then, you wouldn't have your wonderful children.'

'Absolutely. You're right,' replied Arian. 'They are the love of my life. And what about you, Beatrice? Who are you going to kiss at midnight?'

'Please don't! I don't want to have to think about that. Another New Year on my own. That will have to be my New Year's resolution; more sex,' Beatrice said.

It was nowhere near midnight, but they both wanted to kiss each other so badly, as if their entire happiness in the new year depended on it. Arian held Beatrice's hands. 'You'd better go back inside. You must be freezing,' he said. He kissed her slowly on her cheek, collected George, and Beatrice watched the two of them walk away.

It wasn't a kiss at midnight, but it felt like a midnight kiss. She sighed.

Chapter 11

'Beatrice, please allow me to introduce you to Teddy.'

One day, out of the blue, a cheerful, energetic boy arrived at the hotel. It was hard for Beatrice not to notice him as he walked up to Arian. He looked younger and shorter than him, but he walked fast, and he had a sort of confidence about him that told Beatrice the entire story of their past.

They met when they were very young, went to the same school, and they knew everything about each other. Teddy was the one who invented all the trouble they got themselves into, and getting them out of it, with his charms, Arian was able to do.

'Hi, you are the first person over the age of two that Arian has brought into the hotel,' said Beatrice, making an innocent observation.

'Well, I've known him longer than his wife,' was Teddy's reply, to Beatrice's surprise.

On occasions, Arian liked to talk about his life before his marriage. He used to have the most fun, or the most fun for Beatrice, who, on the other hand, never used to get herself into any menace. She was into her career too much. Work completely overtook her life without her ever noticing how much. She loved listening to Arian telling her countless stories about his best friend, Teddy, and how the two of them used to get into trouble while charming the ladies.

Beatrice sat down on a chair next to them. Without looking at them, she took great pleasure in listening to their casual chat. It was the first time she found Arian really comfortable in the company of somebody else other than herself. The two of them were laughing like teenagers.

After Teddy left, Arian and Beatrice had a coffee together. 'Teddy is my oldest friend, and we know everything about each other.'

Unable to tell how and when the conversation started to become more personal, Beatrice was not at all surprised to hear how much Teddy liked to spend his time around beautiful women. He liked them, but he wasn't too keen on becoming committed to them. If a girl got too emotional and needy, that would be it for Teddy.

'He's never been in love before,' said Beatrice, so sure she was able to read him.

Teddy liked to swear a lot. He had already swore in front of Beatrice, and he had only just met her. It was clear to her, in Teddy's company, Arian was able to behave in whatever manner. He didn't need to watch what he was saying. His children, who he had to set an example for, weren't there, and his wife wasn't around either telling him what to do.

'I work really hard to be a good husband.' In his voice, Beatrice felt an entire world's sadness.

'Have you seen the news, Beatrice?' asked Nita as she entered the room. She was almost running. 'I'm so worried about this virus in China,' she continued, without taking a breath. Nita was always up to date with what was going on around the world.

'No, I don't think I did, but I wouldn't worry about it. I'm sure they have it under control.' Beatrice stressed it was nothing for Nita to worry about at all. 'So, I booked you in to complete your review next week. Does that work for you?'

'It's perfect, Beatrice, thank you.'

Beatrice and Nita had worked together for about a year now. Nita would tell Beatrice every week how much she felt her influence in her growth, and how grateful she was for it. Beatrice didn't have the easiest times with Nita. With it being her first management role, she did need to guide her a lot in her managerial behaviour. But the fruits of her hard work were all the sweeter. Beatrice felt how much she wanted to make her feel proud every day and even if she had to be there for her to dictate the steps, when she asked her to do something, she knew Nita would get on with it with her best intent.

When Beatrice turned back to continue her conversation with Arian, to her biggest surprise, she noticed he had already left.

* * *

'So, what are you doing today?'

'Nothing. Well, I have a couple of friends coming over for dinner tonight, but apart from that, I have no other plans,' said Beatrice over the phone.

'Excellent. George and I decided to take you out for a birthday walk.'

Arian managed to get a postcode out of Beatrice and within an hour, father and son were standing on her doorstep rearranging their outfits.

Beatrice grabbed her boots and a poncho. With the sun shining since the morning, it was a warmer day, but there were still some puddles around from the overnight rain. Arian was wearing his high collar black coat. It gave him the most graceful look, Beatrice always thought. They walked towards the end of the road where there was a little playground. It was a weekday with no other people around. Arian let little George wander about.

They didn't stay for long, but with every minute they spent together, Beatrice could feel the affections they had for each other. Out of the two of them Arian was probably the more confident leading conversations.

When he wasn't sure what to say, however, he turned to his little boy, and he made him smile with a funny facial expression.

Beatrice was ever so nervous around little George. Between father and son, she could feel the most incredible bond. She didn't want to scare him off. When she tried to make a connection, with every attempt, George would run to his father and hide behind his legs.

Beatrice was usually particularly good with children, but with Arian being so charming, and eager to make her happy on her birthday, she really didn't know how to handle the situation. She kept smiling and answering his questions. That was not like her. She didn't understand what was happening to her. She looked down at her hands and found them shaking. It was like her body and soul were captured with no chance for escaping.

'Would you like to come in for a cup of coffee?' she asked, standing outside her front door.'

'No thank you. George is getting a little tired; it's time for us to go home.'

* * *

'And what about the British people that were in Wuhan?' asked Beatrice.

'They were offered to return to the UK by the government,' replied Ollie.

For their pre-dinner drinks and half of their evening meal, Beatrice and her friends spent talking about the terrible news in China of a virus outbreak. British Airways suspended all flights to and from the area, and the British people trapped in Wuhan were offered repatriation, it was said in the media.

'There are now three confirmed cases in the UK as well, did you know?' asked Marilena.

It was no longer a topic that didn't interest public opinion and many households had now started talking about the virus on a more regular basis with their companions. It began to scare people. The media have started to recognise the importance of keeping people updated. Virus updates have become more and more regular among news bulletins. It didn't, however, seem like it was something governments couldn't control, and not worthwhile spending the entire birthday dinner talking about, for sure.

'I can't believe you didn't invite him for dinner,' Marilena stated with a shock, ready to change the conversation. She always enjoyed emphasizing how thunderstruck she was.

'How could I?' asked Beatrice rhetorically. 'Oh, by the way, would you and your wife want to come over for dinner tonight?' She was making fun of her own unbearable situation. Deep down, however, she wanted him to be there. More than anything she could think of. 'Either way, I got to see him during the day.'

'Here's to Beatrice, who will never be happy in her entire life because she is too afraid to go for what she wants.' Marilena raised her glass and continued parodying Beatrice's life.

'I just have this terrible feeling that he's incredibly unhappy,' said Beatrice. 'And I'm being a good girl for what? So that this remarkable man, a true gentleman, can carry on living his life broken-hearted?'

'A complete and utter waste,' said Marilena, 'if you were to ask me.'

Chapter 12

February the 14th has always been one of the busiest days in the hotel. Loved up couples arrived from around the country for a relaxing weekend. Beatrice didn't mind the whole parade. She did feel quite fed up with the fact that, once again, she had no boyfriend with whom she could celebrate. It was an easy day to plan for. The guests were going to be happy; of that, everybody was sure. The team used to place their bets on the number of last-minute cancellations, and the number of no-shows. 'Come on! A cancellation is just a fight. That, they can still survive. We'll see them next year. The no-shows, they're the real divorcers.' It was something they all laughed about.

As always, the day went smoothly and with some harmony among the team. The room was decorated in red, making the entire building looking sexy. This year, it was on a Friday. Beatrice and Arian haven't seen each other all week. They didn't speak on the phone either. Arian did call Beatrice for some ridiculous reason on Valentine's Day, however. So ridiculous, Beatrice couldn't even remember the point of the call. She resisted the need to talk to him for hours, and she quickly found a reason to hang up the phone.

It was already Sunday by the time they were in the same room together. There was an uncomfortable tension between them from the second they said hello to each other. Beatrice couldn't understand what this tension was, she tried to keep out of Arian's way, and she tried quietly to get on with her job.

Arian always had this amazing, yet so aggravating to Beatrice, strength to keep silent. Today especially, she wanted nothing more than for him to talk, but he never did. It was almost like he knew that she would break at some point, and eventually, of course, Beatrice did. 'I need you to explain your behaviour towards me, Arian, I don't understand why you are behaving so edgy with me all of a sudden,' said Beatrice with her eyes almost in tears. In tears from anger more than anything else, so she believed.

'I don't know what you mean, Beatrice. I did nothing to upset you. You are the one who's been angry with me from the moment I saw you.'

Beatrice was never any good at hiding her emotions. If she didn't say it with her words, her face told everybody around how she was feeling. It was the first time, however, that she saw Arian angry. She could tell he was upset sometimes, but he always tried to be positive and cheerful in her company. She didn't know what to do, and how to handle his abrupt and almost attacking response. She felt it was best to leave it as it was. She was even more confused as to why and how the two of them ended up so out of tune. The one thing she always knew was that, no matter what she'd say or do, Arian would be sure to approve. He was almost like an admirer to her. She felt, in his opinion, she could never do anything wrong.

Until now.

She spent the entire day smiling at people trying to hide how she was feeling. If Arian went one way, Beatrice went the other. From a distance, however, he never took his eyes of her. While, on the other hand, Beatrice was afraid. She was afraid that she would find out something she didn't want to know about if she dared to look at him again.

Arian was a polite man with good manners. He didn't feel comfortable leaving a conversation on a negative note, certainly not with someone he obviously cared about. To him, Beatrice wasn't just a line manager at that point. She was this incredibly talented woman who was somehow still single, and in need of his support. He could feel how much he was needed by her. Almost every day. Today, he could tell Beatrice was merely trying, and failing, to hide how much she wanted his company. Any other day he would let her suffer longer, but it was already the end of the evening, with only the two of them left in the building. He chose curtesy, and, mercifully, he decided to speak. 'Are you feeling any better?' he asked most politely.

'Not really,' replied Beatrice. 'I'm not used to being in the same room with you and at the same time not able to talk to you. I don't know what I have done. You came in with a funny mood, and I don't understand it,' she continued.

'My mood earlier had nothing to do with you. It was to do with... Never mind. It's nothing to trouble you with.'

Beatrice had a feeling that he was right. It was nothing to do with her, and it was none of her business. She couldn't help but think that it was a matter between him and his Mrs. 'Well, I don't like it. You are anxious and agitated. I like it when we are happy together. Those are my best days. I love them the most. I don't know who this person is. Shaking and rushing, trying to convince everybody how happy he is. I can see through that. You don't fool me. I can distinguish between the happy Arian and the one I feel nothing for, except pitty. Now, I must go, it's not my place to tell you what to do. But there is one thing I want you to know. I've never been as happy in my entire life, as I was…'

'Beatrice, wait!' Arian cried.

It was too late. She was already out the door, battling with her tears.

Chapter 13

Beatrice loved her job. As the leader of a team, she had the opportunity to look after the needs of others. She enjoyed making people understand how they could improve their calling, which, in her mind, was actually helping them live a happy and successful life. Her feedbacks were always inspiring, and they helped the character developments of the individuals. Even when she wasn't keen on a particular performance, she gave people the extra time they needed to make necessary improvements. She was encouraging progress, rather than cutting wings, and wasting her time and money on hiring replacements. She believed in equal opportunity and she believed in equal treatment.

When she delivered a successful event, her reward was the happiness of her guests. She didn't work for money, she worked to make people happy. For her, a perfect day at work was filled with delighted guests and inspired and motivated team members.

As a humanitarian, she cared a lot about people and she didn't manage to get a good night of sleep since the night she fell out with Arian. She was disappointed that she couldn't keep her feelings to herself. Her actions, she considered to be needy and self-centred.

For weeks, she did everything in her power to avoid him. When he needed her help with something she fabricated an excuse why she didn't have the time for him. It wasn't often that she dared to even look at him. She was too embarrassed.

Arian, on the other hand, watched her every move. When he spotted her struggling with a heavy task, he was there within seconds to help her out.

Beatrice could try to avoid him all she wanted, but her mind never became free of him. She was thinking about him every minute of every day. She typed and deleted messages addressed to him. On occasion, she dialled his number and hung up instantly.

'When did it become spring?' Standing by the window in her living room, Beatrice was admiring the trees around the neighbourhood already in full bloom.

Beatrice was a busy girl. Without her ever knowing how much she was missing, she let the world run by her. On occasion, she stopped for a moment wondering what it would be like if she could rewind her life and start it all over. Some days she wished she cared less about work and more about the pleasures of life she never had the time to endeavour. Today, it was one of those days.

'The prime minister advises people not to visit pubs and restaurants.' The newsreader interrupted Beatrice's muse. She walked away from the window, sat down on her couch, and turned up the volume. 'The prime minister urges people to take his advice seriously. People should avoid non-essential travel. When possible, people should work from home and avoid visiting social venues.'

At that moment, Beatrice had a terrible feeling. 'What good does it do, if people stop eating out, to have a career in hospitality. All the hard work and the missed opportunities for building a family would be worthless. This cannot be happening.'

She got dressed in the shortest possible time and drove into work with haste. On her approach to the building, she saw every car, one after the other, driving away. At reception, people were checking out, one by one. Beatrice couldn't believe what was happening. 'What's going on?' she asked the receptionist.

'Everybody is scared. After the prime minister's speech, they are all checking out,' the receptionist said.

Faster than her usual pace, Beatrice continued to make her way inside the hotel. 'Nita, I have a call with the board in an hour. Could you keep the team together until then?'

'Of course. We have no events until the weekend, it will only be a matter of tonight's dinner for anyone who is staying at the hotel.'

'Thanks. I'll be in the office if you need me,' Beatrice said.

As she sat down at her desk, she reached for her phone and saw a missed call from Arian. She did think about calling him back, but after a long pause, she decided to put her phone down instead. She was afraid that the moment she heard his soothing voice she would lose her strength. Right now, she could not afford to do that. She needed to delegate and direct. An entire team was relying on her cool headedness. To her, the ability to collapse in despair was a luxury, and not available to team leaders.

Without further deliberations, she opened up her laptop and logged into a google call. It wasn't the first time the company organised a video call when they needed to brief every manager on the same information. On a certain level, management had got used to it by now. Today, it was different. The uncertainty of what was going to happen made everybody feel on edge. The board gave instructions to keep minimum number of staff on; just what was needed to serve tonight's dinner and only management was required from the day after next. *OK, it isn't so bad,* thought Beatrice, *the worst that could happen is that we will all take a few weeks off.*

The last time Beatrice had a week off from work was the time Marilena took her on a Mediterranean beach resort. She meant it as a present to celebrate her own achievements. Achievements, which she believed could not have happened without Beatrice's endorsement. Beatrice considered it to be the greatest gesture and she didn't find it in her heart to reject her. Happily, as she had the most amazing time. She couldn't understand why she didn't go on holidays herself at least some of the times. She liked to be busy. Being at work gave her the momentum she needed to get on with her life. Work was her master plan. She never waited to gain motivation to start a task, motivation snuck up on her the moment she began. And then, she was on fire. The more she had to do, the more motivated she became. Not having anything to do was when Beatrice felt lost and didn't know how to behave. 'I can do this,' she said out loud as she stood up from her desk. She rearranged her outfit and walked out of the room with confidence.

Chapter 14

The next couple of days everybody spent in the dark, not knowing what was going to happen. Beatrice never felt more uncertain. Even though she was a collected person, who could have the best attitude under pressure, and the ability to attack every obstacle without panic, she was now astounded. She didn't know what her next steps would be. She was worried about her people; she was worried about her family. It was a matter surrounding the globe. With nowhere to hide, without salvage, and without hope. Reporters stopped talking about anything else. People spent their days on their phones. They were either talking to their friends and relatives, worrying about their health, or talking to their colleagues about possible ways of keeping their workload moving ahead.

'Nita, I need you to call and cancel all of our restaurant reservations for tomorrow and the weekend. We have to completely close today, by midnight at the latest.'

A lot of work had begun.

The assistant managers were organising stock, while Beatrice was calling up team members making sure they were well looked after. She briefed them on as much she could. Furniture was covered with big white sheets, curtains got closed in every room, silverware was polished and stored in locked cupboards. By the end of the night, the entire hotel looked like a palace that had been abandoned.

Beatrice looked at her phone. She remembered Arian, and how she never called him back. Sitting at one of the tables in the restaurant, she decided to make a plan. She believed the best way to know what the next day would bring, was by being prepared. Being there all by herself started to make her feel really anxious. Anxious about the country in full lockdown, and about not having a job to escape to for a while.

Beatrice landed a job straight after her graduation and she hasn't spent a week unemployed ever since. The idea of staying at home was unfamiliar to her, and somewhat frightening. She knew she wasn't going to see her family for a while, and she knew she wasn't going to have an easy time surviving.

As she sat there by herself, thinking more than it was good for her, she started to have more and more negative thoughts. She remembered the times she worked with Logan. With Logan, she always felt safe. He was, after all, more than impressed with Beatrice's work ethic, talents, and capabilities. He gave her an opportunity when she asked for one and Beatrice was forever grateful for it. She believed in his superior qualities. Among those, she gave special attention to his ability to calculate every situation in advance and make clever decisions on how to proceed. Logan always knew, better than Beatrice herself, what was good for her.

'Listen to me, you know I'm right,' he used to say to her every time.

Tonight, more than ever, Beatrice wished Logan was there to tell her everything was going to be all right. She looked at her phone with tears accumulating in the corner of her eyes.

'I don't know what I'm going to do,' she typed.

'No one does,' replied Logan within seconds, to Beatrice's surprise. Another message appeared on her screen before she could reply. 'It will all be all right, and as I always say – you know I'm right.'

Without any time to scrutinise what just happened – Beatrice always overanalysed every conversation she had with Logan – Arian suddenly appeared in front of her eyes. Falling straight into his arms, it was like they had never spent a day apart. Both their hearts filled with joy; they made their way towards the drawing room. Arian politely held the door open for her. Letting her walk in front of him, he invited her to sit down on the couch beside him.

'Real gentlemen always walk after their ladies,' he said, most profoundly. 'It's true, I was taught that, I know everything about chivalry. I didn't enjoy quarrelling with you the last time.'

'Me neither,' said Beatrice, thinking the couch comfortable, the subject of conversation not so much. To her liking, however, that was it. They both stated how much they disliked falling out, and they were now content and happy to leave the topic behind.

'It all looks so deserted,' Arian said as he looked around.

They talked about the prime minister's announcement, and how they thought everyone had been hearing about this killer virus for months, but nobody had taken it seriously. Arian knew every little detail about what was going on in the world. It was almost like he knew what was about to happen while everybody else was left confused. He was a highly intelligent man who understood world politics and took interest in current affairs. He could have easily been a politician or, better yet, one of the Lord Justices of the court system. He was familiar with the law and the country's policies. Beatrice learnt something new every time she had a conversation with him.

'This is just the first phase. More likely than not, there will be at least a couple more after this.'

'What do you mean? We'll have to stay at home for a couple of weeks, that's all. That's my hope at least.'

'Do not listen to me, my darling Beatrice, I am sure you are right. There is no reason for you not to be. Please keep your hope. What else is left for us to do without our hopes?'

'How can you say such beautiful things at such terrible times?' asked Beatrice.

'It is my duty, my dear,' Arian replied.

After they finished their coffees, Beatrice went upstairs to collect her belongings. She never had coffee after four in the afternoon, except when she was with Arian. Coffee made her stay awake all night, but when she was with him, she didn't mind staying awake. As she lay in bed, she enjoyed daydreaming about Arian. It was the only time she could hold his hand, the only time she could kiss his lips, and the only time she could tell him how she felt.

After a few awkward sentences, that were clearly stated for no other reason than to stall while they could examine each other's body language, Arian leaned closer and kissed Beatrice goodbye. While holding her close to his body, she could smell his aftershave. It was killing her not knowing when she was going to see him again. She wanted to make the moment last. 'Goodbye, my darling Beatrice, and do take care of yourself.' He had to almost scrape her off from under his arms.

Chapter 15

The world panicked. The prime minister didn't allow people to leave their houses. Everybody had to stay at home unless they were shopping for essentials. Hospital beds were full of infected people, not leaving room for the very ill, or the very injured. There were not enough oxygen masks, not enough ventilators, not enough nurses to deal with the pressure. It was like a war without guns, with the need for everybody to pull together. People volunteered to help out. They helped build hospitals. Within the space of a few days, entire wards were put up from scratch. Ventilators were ordered to be made by manufacturers. Doctors and nurses were working without sleep. It was a time not seen in many years. Country borders were closed. The entire world became distraught.

'Yes, distraught,' said Beatrice over the phone. 'Where are you?'

'I'm at the village store. I need to get something for George. He isn't feeling very well,' said Arian. 'I fear this season won't be the same for many of us.'

'I believe you're right. Do you have any plans on how you might get yourself through it all?' Beatrice asked.

'I'm going to fix things around the house. Things, that usually get left behind when we are busy living our lives. I must get on, my darling Beatrice, I bid you goodbye.'

Arian called Beatrice almost every week. His calls were long, and he never ran out of things to say without ever taking part in unkind gossiping. He believed bad-mouthing would defeat a true gentleman's duty. The duty to protect his own and others' integrity.

Every day, Arian had a new story about his children. Beatrice liked him as a father, she could listen to his stories about George and Grace hour after hour. He told her how much fun they had when they were in the garden, caught up in the rain while playing hide and seek, and about the bedtime stories he read to them when they were getting ready to go to sleep. Arian was a great storyteller. He had the ability to make his stories funny, interesting and the most admirable to those ardently listening.

Four weeks into the national lockdown and Beatrice started to feel very weak. Over the phone, she could still talk to him for hours but in between his phone calls, she preferred to spend her time sleeping.

'Good afternoon, darling Beatrice. Are you keeping well?'

'I was so looking forward to your call, I'm fine thank you.' Beatrice was too ashamed to admit she was unwell.

'Promise me that you are keeping yourself busy. You must get things done. You must have a sense of purpose. You must have a feeling of achievement. You need to go outside, speak to your neighbours, get some fresh air.' Arian took it upon himself to look after Beatrice. He wanted to make sure she wasn't feeling lonely. Most of the time he sounded like an experienced therapist. With his wisdom and kindness, every one of his words were healing Beatrice.

'I've been meaning to ask you, Arian, have you been in touch with any of the team?'

'No, I haven't.'

'Well, I'm always here for you,' said Beatrice. 'And I thank you for being here for me. Please call me as soon as you can!'

'I should be delighted.'

Beatrice desperately felt the need for a sudden change of habits. Every day she felt more and more lethargic. Her motivation, which came so naturally to her by being at work and around other people, was now nowhere to be seen. She enjoyed her first cup of coffee in the morning. The second bored her terribly. She waited until she got really hungry before she started to prepare her lunch. The feeling of an empty stomach was the greatest motivation for her to get up. After that, she had a nap. With Netflix on, quietly in the background, she was able to fall asleep again. She closed her eyes and daydreamed about a better life. A life in the arms of Arian. *Fixing things around the house. That's what he is doing at this moment. Maybe I should get up and do that myself*, Beatrice thought to herself. Arian was able to make Beatrice see the good in the world that many people failed to notice. *He said I should make a plan. I'm going to do that. I'm going to make a plan for myself.*

She folded her blanket and turned off Netflix. She looked around the house in every cupboard and every drawer until she found it. A Christmas present from Frances. A blank notepad. She got excited and she started to use it. Every day she planned to work on a few bits. She made a list, and she changed her eating habits. Beatrice never used to have any breakfast. Her first meal every day was around midday. She couldn't help but remember what Arian used to say. 'A healthy mind is the product of a healthy body. Breakfast is the most important meal of the day.'

She started to think about what she ate more carefully, and she started to eat in the mornings. She never cared about her weight before. The large amount of stress that came with her job always kept her in good shape. After one month in the house, however, she started to notice some gain. She decided to include one hour of exercise on her to-do list every day. For keeping sane, she included an evening walk. Before, she used to enjoy walking alone. She worked on the house on occasion. That was the time she could do something creative.

'You need to do something productive, something creative and something relaxing every day.' Another thing Arian told her one day.

'Relaxing? That's not something I'm good with.'

For Beatrice, relaxing meant listening to her music while she was driving. Now she remembered when she was a student, she used to love reading. She loved second-hand books with inscriptions. It was like being a part of somebody else's story, she always thought. She decided to start reading again.

And that's how it was.

Her days went by, one after the other. Her favourites were the ones when Arian called her. They could spend hours and hours talking about their errands. When Beatrice complained that he didn't call sooner, Arian explained, 'This way we have more to say to each other and we can talk for longer.'

Chapter 16

It was the warmest spring in many years. The trees were blooming, and the sun was shining almost every day. People enjoyed working in their gardens. The streets of the neighbourhood used to be silent but now they were filled with dog walkers. Every household had their dinners together every day. Before, it was almost unheard of. People who lived on the same street got to know each other. A real togetherness was felt by all. Sons helped their fathers and daughters helped their mothers.

Beatrice was alone. More alone than ever before.

'What do you have in mind?' asked Arian.

'I was thinking about a two-meter-long bench.'

Like a child on Christmas Day, was the kind of excitement Beatrice could feel. She couldn't remember the last time she laid eyes on Arian, and she wanted nothing more than to see him again. After she hung up the phone, in no time at all, she was merrily on the road. It was not the warmest day in May, but the skies were clear with no clouds around threatening to rain.

'My darling Beatrice. It is so good to see you. So good to see you,' said Arian as he rushed towards her.

She didn't even have time to think about whether it was OK to hug him, in less than a second, she stood there with her arms around him. It was a wonderful feeling. She remembered the butterflies. *Yes, definitely still there,* she thought to herself. *Just like every other time.*

She couldn't believe what was happening to her. There he was, in front of her eyes, this handsome young man with manners she only ever read about in novels, and he was excited to see her. To Beatrice, it was crystal clear how happy he was to meet with her. *He couldn't possibly believe I don't feel it,* she kept wondering. Beatrice never really understood what the girls meant when they were talking about The One, The Right Guy, The Mr Big, but with Arian she felt this could be it.

'What I miss the most about being in a relationship is being kissed,' said Beatrice, blushing.

She could talk to Arian about everything, but when it was about her deepest feelings, she thought it was embarrassing. Those conversations, she loved the most, however. It was incredibly delightful for her to watch Arian become so uncomfortable. They talked about the different sexual positions and which of those they found the most admirable. Beatrice never revealed such deep emotions to anybody else before. Not even Miss Marilena was ever entertained by her erotic thoughts.

'Once this lockdown is over, I am definitely getting a boyfriend,' said Beatrice. 'And do you know what? He will be the luckiest man in the world. I'll let him do anything he wants.' They both smiled. How red their faces suddenly became; it was impossible for them to hide.

For the best part of the afternoon, they sat under a tree in the hotel gardens, talking about their hopes, fears, passions, and desires. They sat close enough to feel the chemistry, even though they were on a bench, two meters long precisely.

'I'll help you find a boyfriend,' said Arian, eagerly and confidently.

'He needs to understand women, know the importance of intellectual conversations, have a respectable job, not be married, know how to wear a suit, drive a nice car, have good table etiquette, a good sense of humour, and he must also be sexually active with the desire to experiment,' said Beatrice without taking a breath.

'Nice list of duties there. I am a great agent but not a wizard,' teased Arian.

'And how's Teddy?' she asked, trying to move away from the conversation.

'When I'm with Teddy, I feel like I've been given the gift of freedom.'

Arian was the happiest of all when he was talking about Teddy. He would make the funniest comments, and Beatrice would listen to him for hours as he told her about a million joyful stories. Teddy called Arian twice daily. Beatrice didn't have a clue what they could talk about every day, but many a time, she was there when he called late in the evenings.

Teddy was a kind man. A cheerful, energetic man, who took it upon himself to look after Arian. On occasions, when Arian answered the phone, Teddy would start to sing without as much as a "Hello". Beatrice never understood the lyrics, but she could tell his songs were happy and ecstatic.

Arian always talked about Teddy with affection and amity. Beatrice had a loving feeling for him, and she wished they were in a closer proximity. If they could meet more often, she knew they would become good friends. If not for anything else, then for the shared love they had for Arian. 'Who said Teddy would want to speak with you?' Arian used to tease Beatrice every time she warned she would call Teddy when Arian declined to tell her something. Arian liked to stay private, and he never shared more information than it was good for him. Beatrice was able to read many things, but because of her slightly paranoid and overthinking personality, sometimes she wished she wouldn't have to keep on guessing.

Teddy will tell, I will make sure of it, Beatrice thought to herself.

After they shared their joys, they decided to share their sorrows next. Arian talked about little George not feeling very well, and Beatrice told Arian how in the last few weeks she felt lonely and nothing else. Beatrice was the kind of girl that liked to be left alone but she didn't like to feel lonely. She was the happiest next to Arian, but she knew that she would have to go home eventually.

Home.

She was fed up with being at home. Nothing ever happened at home. The grass was green, and the flowers were blooming, she did have enough time to look after them, after all. She completed her to-do lists, hitting every deadline, placing her individual precision into every detail. It was the most boring thing she could do. Ever. She wanted to be free, she wanted to travel, she wanted to do something crazy, anything that was out of the ordinary. Otherwise, she would go mad. That was it. The time was coming when she could take it no longer. She wanted to scream from the top of her lung, she wanted everybody to hear how miserable she was. A life imprisoned was no life at all. And that's exactly how she felt. She felt like she was in a prison, with her initials carved onto the wall.

I will definitely come back, thought Beatrice after leaving the gardens.

She got inside her car, and with tears in her eyes, she drove away. On her way home, she kept thinking about Teddy. How was it that she had such loving feelings for someone she met once, and had never even talked to since. It was obvious to her how much Arian loved him.

That was the only explanation. He loved Teddy and it was his love for him that Beatrice could feel in every story.

That day, especially, Beatrice felt Arian's sadness. Her feelings of imprisonment was shared by him. She could tell, in all fairness.

'Wow, I've never seen anything like this before,' said Beatrice looking at the side of the road. With no other cars around, the entire country seemed to have been overtaken by wild animals. They were too afraid of the noise before. Now, even birds were flying low.

Chapter 17

Walking by the edge of the village, Beatrice was able to let her mind travel to all sorts of different places. Today she kept thinking about Arian's brutal statement. The second or third day he met her, he told her how it was her own decision to live a life without sex and that he would never be able to do that. Sex was a natural need of a healthy body, and he found it hard to accept that a beautiful woman like Beatrice would choose a life without it. 'I didn't choose a life without sex; I do meet men sometimes,' Beatrice said.

She really didn't meet men on a regular basis and especially not for the purpose of sexual satisfaction. In fact, she couldn't remember the last time she had sex, but she was not going to let Arian know that. 'I cannot believe you chose a life without love. I would never be able to do that,' Beatrice said. 'I'm always in love. Every minute of every day. In fact, I'm in love today.'

The thought of Arian, or the feeling of the cool breeze touching her skin, made Beatrice feel horny. She didn't know exactly what it was that made her want to have sex so much, but she couldn't think about anything else during her evening walk.

***

'I'm at your front door,' whispered Arian over the phone.

'What? What do you mean you're at my front door?' asked Beatrice.

'Let me in and I will explain. Be quick, someone might see me.'

'Arian, it's a national lockdown, you're not supposed to visit me,' said Beatrice as she opened the door.

'Staying away from you was too much, I couldn't do it anymore.'

'It's three o'clock in the morning. You'll get me into trouble.'

Arian walked away from the front door and rushed to the other end of the room with haste. 'Come closer, Beatrice!' He looked deeply into her eyes and with one of his hands, he gently stroked her face.

Not knowing what to say to him, Beatrice stood there silently. She let him lean in and kiss her lips. He opened her dressing gown under which she was completely naked. He pushed it slowly off her shoulders, letting it fall onto the floor. He stopped kissing her; he wanted to explore her naked body. As she stood there in front of him, she never felt happier. This time with both of his hands, he touched her face again. Moving them slowly down her shoulders and her breasts, he could feel her heart beat faster and faster. He pulled her closer by her waist, her racing heart he wanted to embrace. He turned her body towards the bedroom door. He wanted her to go there, Beatrice was sure. As she walked in front of him with grace, he watched her naked legs. Once inside the bedroom, she laid on the bed. Together with his pants, he slowly pulled his trousers halfway down his legs. While looking deep into her eyes he gently moved on top of her. Without any further foreplay, he was instantly inside of her.

Beatrice jumped from the sudden sensation and opened her eyes. She realised she was dreaming.

She was dreaming about Arian and for the first time it was erotic. As she closed her eyes, she was still turned on, she could feel it. The more she let herself think about her dream, the more excited she became. With one of her hands, she reached inside her pants and she didn't need to leave it there for too long before she came.

The next morning Beatrice woke up with a smile; a smile, and an embarrassment. It wasn't the first time she touched herself, of course, but it was the first time she did it while she was thinking about Arian. *How am I going to look into his eyes?* She blushed from her own pondering.

During the entire day and most of the evening, Beatrice couldn't keep her hands off of her body. She did it on her couch, she did it in her bedroom, she did it in five different places. It was the first day she missed her evening walk. She didn't cook a full meal. She had a cold plate on her couch and she reached for her phone.

'I miss having a boyfriend,' said Beatrice, feeling depressed and lonely. 'What are you up to at home? How are you keeping busy?'

'Well, you know me, I always have some crazy ideas. I'm thinking about starting my own business.'

Marilena found it difficult to find herself a wedding dress that suited her personality and elegance. She looked everywhere in the neighbourhood but anything that was worth considering, in her opinion, cost a fortune. She was thinking about opening her own bridal shop instead. She started to work on it online, and she was planning to open a small boutique after travelling and visiting local shops and businesses were once again allowed.

'But please don't tell anybody yet!'

Beatrice was wondering whether what was going on around the world would change the mindset of everybody. Up until now, many people believed that working in hospitality would provide them with job security. Nobody ever imagined a time when there would be no restaurants, coffee shops or hotels open on the highstreets. It was a real eye-opener for many.

As she hung up the phone, Beatrice felt even more lethargic. She needed to go out and see people, she needed to be kissed. She needed to be hugged. She was desperate for someone to make her laugh. People had stopped telling her jokes by now. It was like laughing was no longer an option. Every conversation with her friends and family was predominantly about concerns. Concerns about their wellbeing, financial and otherwise. The phrase "take care" got replaced by "stay safe". Although love was purposefully made apparent in every medium, and the people of the country seemed to become closer than ever before, Beatrice couldn't help but feel lonely. 'Another night in with myself,' she said, sighing.

Chapter 18

'What do you mean she's having the baby? It's too soon, isn't it?' asked Beatrice.

'Yes, it is. Six weeks too soon, to be exact,' replied Nick. 'I just wanted to let you know that we'll have another baby by the time the sun rises tomorrow.'

'Call me as soon as you can, I probably won't sleep a wink.'

Beatrice hadn't see her brother and his family since Christmas. It was awfully hard for her not being able to see them, especially the little ones. Frances was still working in the hospital, understaffed, and pregnant.

'How do you do it?'

'This is what med school prepared us for,' she would say to everyone who had asked her.

Beatrice, ever since she was a little girl, fainted at the sight of blood. On occasions, it was enough for her to just think of the sight of it and she already felt nauseous and dizzy. She attended numerous first aid courses and she was one of the first-aiders at the hotel. Luckily, she never actually had to deal with any accidents as of yet. She always knew she would be the first one to pass out. It was one of the many reasons that she admired all the hospital workers. They had the ability to keep themselves together in an emergency. Not to mention the mental difficulty of the job. That was even more admirable. Having to watch people in distress must have been the hardest thing of all.

* * *

The next day, Beatrice felt the most enthusiastic she had felt in months. There was a new baby in the family. Mother and child were both well and safe and her brother was the proudest he could ever be. It was the middle of June. The weather was beautiful. Filled with hope and aspiration, Beatrice kept herself busy all day. She kept checking the time since the moment she was awake. She knew, as soon as the sun went down, she would drive into Autumn Leaves. She could see the light at the end of a dark and dreadful tunnel. She could feel freedom. She could feel the end of a period of her feeling miserable. It was the happiest day for Beatrice, and she was eager to make the most of it. At exactly 9pm, she left her house excitedly.

The hotel looked unchanged. Almost three full months had went by since, in that same spot, she was kissing Arian goodbye. As she walked in through the front door, she could smell the smell of neglect almost instantly. She went into the drawing room and opened a window. Walking around the room, she touched every piece of furniture now covered with a white throw. The room was cold, and it gave Beatrice a feeling of sorrow. She remembered her times in the hotel. Every conversation, every meeting, and every appointment. She remembered the night she sat on the couch next to Arian.

She walked towards the ballroom door. The heavy oak double doors were never kept closed before. To pull them open, she needed to collect all her strengths. Behind them, she imagined glitter and luminescence. A room full of people dancing. Chandeliers sparkling. Men in tuxedos and women in glamorous gowns. Team members handing out champagne to the crowd. After only one blink, her image disappeared. The room was empty, the double doors revealed. It never felt bigger and more powerful. Whilst looking around, Beatrice made her way towards the dance floor. When she got to the middle, she turned back to the door. She saw Arian standing there, more handsome than ever before.

'What are you doing here?' asked Beatrice.

'I saw you come inside so I followed you,' Arian replied.

Without saying another word, he slowly walked up to her. He held out his hand and waited for her to accept. Lights turned on and music started playing. Within seconds, the two of them were dancing. In the arms of Arian, Beatrice didn't want the moment to end. They danced around the room in merriment. Beatrice kept wondering how it was at all possible that a young man like Arian would know how to dance. Never in her wildest dreams had she imagined that he would know how to lead. When the song finished, Arian thanked

Beatrice. 'Much obliged,' he said, and he walked out of the room with grace.

The next day Beatrice decided to come back to Autumn Leaves.

She was still in her car when Arian appeared on the left. He opened the door and reached for her seatbelt. With Beatrice in his arms, he walked towards the building. Beatrice felt feeble and dizzy. She kept wondering whether she was dreaming. Everything seemed bright, and everything seemed blurry. She wanted nothing more than to be inside. Just like the previous night. In the arms of Arian. Dancing.

Chapter 19

'Hi, you must be Logan. I've heard a lot about you,' said Marilena. 'I'm afraid we can't go inside. It's to do with bringing in bacteria.' Logan's expressions were tired and exhausted. He still kept a clean look and a tidy outfit. Marilena couldn't help but notice. *He must have been through hell*, she thought to herself. *He looks broken-hearted.* 'Have you told her family?'

'I called her brother. They are in hospital themselves. They just had a baby. Can I buy you a coffee?'

With a couple of cappuccinos in their hands, Logan and Marilena sat down on a bench.

'I'm so glad you were there,' said Marilena. 'But I don't understand, were you together? I mean what happened?'

'Beatrice called me a few weeks ago. We had a really nice talk, and I asked her if I could call her sometimes. I was trying to get hold of her last night.'

Logan told Marilena everything. He called Beatrice four times with no answer and that was when he got really worried. He decided to drive to her house to check on Beatrice. He kept knocking on the door and he tried to look through the window. The lights were down, and it seemed like nobody was home. He didn't stop knocking until he could be sure. From the neighbours, he heard a voice. 'She left about an hour ago.'

'Thank you so much, do you know where she went?' Logan saw an old lady look over the fence.

'No, I just saw her through my window. She seemed excited though.'

'Thank you again Mrs... Hmm?'

'Bonington. Mrs Bonington.'

Mrs Bonington was, among her other neighbours, the one Beatrice kept a closer relationship with. She was a sweet lady in her seventies, and she believed it to be her duty to look after Beatrice. Beatrice didn't only find her to be the most interesting person because of her wisdom and experience in life, but she also thought her to be humorous, and someone with a kind heart.

'Thank you, Mrs Bonington. I'm trying to call her but she's not answering her phone. Maybe she drove to the hotel. Let me check there.'

'Please tell her to call me, or else I'll worry.'

'Of course, Mrs Bonington, I will definitely do that,' Logan said.

He got into his car with haste and drove towards
Autumn Leaves. He hadn't been driving for longer than
a few minutes when he saw a car crashed into a tree.
Inside it, unconscious, was Beatrice.

* * *

Logan was a man with unique abilities. He could
stay calm in whatever the circumstances. He was
hopeful, he was reassuring, he was serene. He was an
intelligent man, in a world of mess, still able to see clear.
'Beatrice always thought highly of my ability to keep
cool, but I tell you, Marilena, when I saw her car, I
didn't know what to do. I was scared. I was scared I was
too late. I don't even know how I managed to breathe.'

'Please don't tell me the rest. I keep thinking, if you
weren't there, what could've happened.'

'It's not over yet.'

'But she will recover, isn't that what they said?'

'Yes. What that means, nobody knows yet.'

'Did they tell you when we would be able to visit
her?'

'They will let you know. I gave them your number.'

Logan thought Beatrice needed to be comforted by
someone she was close with. He knew how self-
conscious she always felt whenever she was in his

company. And even if he wanted to see her terribly, he wasn't sure how she would react if the first person she saw was him.

'We can't do much more now. I think I might go home and try to have a rest.'

'You must be knackered,' Marilena said.

'They gave me her keys and her phone. You should take these. Would you speak to her neighbour? I made her a promise.'

'I will go there now. Thank you. Try not to think about it, somehow.'

What a nice man, Marilena said to herself. She was able to see straight away why Beatrice was so hooked up on him all those years.

Chapter 20

'Hey, how are you doing? Are you feeling any better?' asked Marilena, walking up to Beatrice's bed.

'The doctor told me I had an accident.'

Marilena was still at Beatrice's house when the hospital called to say that it was OK for her to visit her. She collected a few things that she thought might be of use to her. She drove back to the hospital with haste.

Marilena was a strong woman. In her opinion, actions defined a person. She was real, she wasn't fake. And that's exactly how she behaved. She told the truth and nothing but the truth. In every situation, in any case. With Beatrice, standing by her hospital bed, she thought it best to talk about the things that were hopeful and blessed.

'Your brother's baby is so beautiful. Look, he sent you a picture.'

'I can't believe I'm an aunty again,' said Beatrice. 'I wish I could visit him,' she continued, feeling lethargic.

'You will. And it will be the most wonderful thing.'

Marilena told Beatrice how nice it was to finally see retail shops open on the highstreets. Soon, they would be able to say the same thing about hospitality buildings. The world was opening up again. In the air, there was an optimistic feeling.

It wasn't easy for Marilena to stay cheerful in front of Beatrice. She wanted to tell her how she looked. Beaten, bruised, and exhausted. That would have been the honest thing. Instead, she kept smiling and picked her topics carefully.

'I'm back at work tomorrow, getting ready for the opening,' she said to her blithely. 'Now, I'd better let you sleep, you look a bit drowsy. But when I come back, I will tell you everything.'

* * *

'Do you think I should go there and see her?' By now, Logan was desperate to be near Beatrice.

'Maybe it would be better to wait a bit. I haven't told her about Arian yet, and I don't know how she will react to it.'

'Marilena, if you don't mind me asking, how come you never met him?'

'Beatrice told me he was married. I figured girls don't date married men in public.'

Marilena was on the phone to Logan, walking up and down the hospital foyer nervously. It was a week after the accident and she was worried about her best friend. Beatrice was recovering well. What made Marilena anxious was telling Beatrice the truth about Arian. When she hung up the phone, she took a deep breath.

'Come in!' said Beatrice.

'Hello, beautiful, and how well you look!' Marilena placed her handbag on a chair and sat down next to Beatrice on the bed. 'I have something I need to tell you.' she started, confident.

'Where is Arian? I need to thank him for saving my life. He's the one who brought me to hospital,' Beatrice replied.

'Arian Froberville was the Viscount of Darlington and he lived with his family during the early twentieth century. They lived at Autumn Leaves House Hotel, which, as you know, was called Darlington Palace back then. The viscount was married to the viscountess, Lady Meredith Froberville, and they had two wonderful children.'

'Why are you telling me this?'

'Arian doesn't exist, Beatrice.' Marilena didn't know how better to tell Beatrice that she made up a person just because she missed being with somebody so tremendously.

'You're wrong, ask people at the hotel. I hired Arian in the autumn, and he has been working with us ever since.'

'I did ask in the hotel, Beatrice. Nita told me that there was a new starter called Adrian last year who impressed you immensely. Only, after a couple of weeks, without notice, he disappeared. Nobody had seen him since.'

'But surely my team told you about Arian.'

'Nobody recalls any man called Arian working at, or visiting, the hotel.'

Beatrice looked towards the window. She was desperately trying to think of an occasion when she saw Arian together with another person. With tears filling up her eyes, not able to come up with one took her by surprise. Until, suddenly, she looked back at Marilena with a hopeful look in her eyes. 'I met his best friend, Teddy,' she said excitedly.

'I don't know what else to tell you, Beatrice,' said Marilena, desperately.

Even Beatrice was now able to see how painful it was for Marilena to keep on talking. She decided to keep quiet and watched Marilena staring down on her bed. Her amazing friend, this remarkable woman, who was never lost for words, now didn't know how to act. She looked sad. She looked like she was struggling with the idea that her good friend, Beatrice, had gone mad. A lunatic, who was imagining people who didn't exist. To Beatrice, the whole thing felt unreal, and disturbing. But the sight of her best friend in pieces, she thought, was even more terrifying. 'I believe you,' she said as she reached out to hold her hand. 'And I know how hard it must have been for you to tell me all that. How's Nita doing?' she asked, determined to change the subject.

'She's doing well with the re-opening,' Marilena said.

Nita took over the entire organisation of the re-opening that everybody was waiting for. On the 4th of July, social venues were finally able to open their doors. The senior teams started to get their workers together. They started to train people. There were plenty of new policies and procedures. Nita stepped into Beatrice's shoes with great confidence. She showed a professional, calm, and ever so eager manner. She wanted to make Beatrice proud. More than ever.

'And what's happening with your wedding?' Beatrice continued her questioning.

'Still postponed,' said Marilena looking sad and irritated. 'Can you believe that I was supposed to be a married woman in less than a month? But let's not talk about it. I've had enough. We're going to have a look at our new boutique tomorrow, and I need you to get well soon. With the planning of the launch party, I'm counting on you. It's going to be fabulous; I'm thinking white dahlias everywhere, I'm thinking pearls and overflowing centrepieces,' said Miss Marilena. Upbeat and optimistic.

Beatrice watched Marilena fall deeply into the details of her plans. She listened to her describe the entire event. As some of the words started to fade away, she noticed her eyes filling up with tears again. Still holding Marilena's hand, she was thinking about her days with Arian. And how this entire time she believed she was loved by a gentleman.

Chapter 21

'We're almost there, hold on, Beatrice, once we're inside you'll feel better, I promise.'

Logan, with Beatrice in his arms, rushed towards the A & E building. Doctors and nurses quickly approached him. Everything was bright and everything was blurry. Beatrice started remembering the accident.

She was lying in her hospital bed the day after Marilena told her about Arian. She remembered leaving her house at sunset. She remembered her excitement. She remembered a beautiful summer night. Out of nowhere, in front of her car, a roebuck staring deep into her eyes.

Beatrice sat up on her bed with caution. On her bedside table there was a greeting card already open: "You gave me such a scare. I cannot wait to see you. Love, Logan."

Beatrice forced herself to think about the night of the accident. *I wasn't with Arian*, she kept telling herself. *I never even made it to the hotel.*

The longer she thought about it, the more she believed Marilena's story about Arian was real. She couldn't recall a time when they were together in other people's company. It always seemed to have been only the two of them. How she was able to see his little boy, and his best friend, Teddy, was even harder for her to understand. She recalled her birthday walk. This time she could see herself walking alone. She recalled her Christmas shopping. On a bench, by the ice rink, on her own, Beatrice was sitting. She remembered her Monday nights. She was eating alone, she realised. The more she forced herself to think about it, the more upset she became. Everything was confused, everything was unclear.

'Hello, Beatrice, are you feeling any better?' said Miss Marilena as she entered.

'I am. I was just thinking about the accident.'

'Don't force it. You look a bit sad.'

'It's just difficult to understand.'

'I'm not going to pretend to know what you're going through, Beatrice, but if you were to ask me, you need to take it gradually. What you need to think about now is that you'll be able to go home finally. I will pick you up tomorrow at three. Now, I'm here to talk to you about Logan, actually.'

'Logan? Why? What do you mean, talk to me?'

'I'm not sure how much you remember, but he was your saviour. He found your car and he brought you to hospital. Not only that, in the last few days he made sure your house wasn't in a mess.'

'Logan is in my house? What's he doing there?'

'He was just checking everything was in order. Tomorrow he'll be there to give you a hand-over.'

Beatrice was thrilled, of course, but unable to hide how nervous she was. Marilena talked about Logan with compassion. She didn't deny her admiration. In the last few days, she talked to him more often than she did with Beatrice. She thought he was kind, considerate, and, towards Beatrice, ever so caring. She thought he was funny and intelligent. They got on well. From the way she talked about him, Beatrice could tell. 'I want you to marry him. And live happily ever after.'

* * *

'Mind the steps but do look at this beautiful day,' Marilena said.

Beatrice was excited to be able to leave the hospital finally. The sky was clear, and the sun was shining. She felt hopeful and excited.

As Marilena pulled up to her cottage, they saw Mrs Bonington and Logan chatting by the garage. The two of them became good friends while Beatrice was away. Mrs Bonington fell in love with Logan, needless to say.

'She needs somebody like you,' she would say to him every time. 'I would feel more comfortable.' She would follow it with a smile.

Logan thought Mrs Bonington was a lovely lady. He would chat to her every day without hesitating.

Marilena decided to make some drinks while Logan sat down in the garden with Beatrice. He organised her patio furniture comfortably, away from the sun, where Beatrice could rest peacefully. Beatrice thought she'd be feeling uneasy, but instead, she never felt more restful and cosy.

'Thank you so much for everything. I don't know how I'm going to return all of this.'

'It's my pleasure. I'm only glad I could help,' Logan said sincerely.

'Did Marilena tell you that I've gone mad?'

'Yes. That's why I was kept at arm's-length.'

'Come on! Enough about that!' Marilena said, entering the garden. 'Nobody is crazy, and nobody's gone mad. It's not like you were talking to yourself. Those conversations only happened in your head. Think of it as daydreaming, and who doesn't do that?'

'But why the viscount? That's what's so hard to understand.'

'You wanted a gentleman.'

'He did sound like a good catch,' Logan said.

'Is that with a hint of jealousy?' Miss Marilena asked teasing.

Beatrice just sat there, looking at him, smiling. 'He was. I mean he really was. You remember, Marilena? It's because of him that I stopped smoking. Without him, I'd be sitting here puffing on a three-inch-stick. And maybe all those conversations at the hotel I imagined to make myself feel better. So desperately wanting to be with somebody. But if you think about it, during lockdown, what would've happened if I didn't have his company? He told me everything I needed to do not to feel lonely. I went for my walks because of him. I started to eat breakfast and I picked my food carefully. I talked to my neighbours and fixed things around the house. If it weren't for him, I would've been sitting on my couch. Arian guided me through it. I can't even imagine what I would've done without him.'

'He did sound like a terrific guy,' Marilena said, smiling.

Beatrice was thinking about Arian for the rest of the evening. *But how was it that I was able to see his little boy and his best friend, Teddy?* She couldn't understand it.

The Viscount Froberville was an actual gentleman living in a mansion. He did everything with the uppermost attention. No wonder Arian was such a great companion. Of course he was so knowledgeable; back in those days, viscounts were given legal positions. Somehow, it still didn't make sense to her. Something was still missing.

Why did he seem so sad? she kept wondering.

Chapter 22

'Are you sure you want to do this?' asked Marilena.

Beatrice was sitting on a bench in Aylesbury in the middle of Market Square. Behind her was the great building of the county hall. She didn't know herself if she was doing the right thing, but she wanted to know more about the Viscount. After she hung up the phone, with her heart pounding, she decided to go inside. 'What harm can it do?' She couldn't decide.

It wasn't difficult for her to get permission. When she was talking to strangers, she always had a charming first impression. The receptionist was the most obliged. Beatrice spent the entire day there. Without coffee and without lunch, she read every archive, every file, and every newspaper. It was the most eye-opening experience of her life. Everyone could see her emotions enfold in her expressions as they were passing by. On occasion, she had tears falling down her cheeks while, many other times, she was heard laughing out loud.

The viscount was born in 1885 into an English upper-middle-class family. He was known by the name Arian Froberville. It was King George the V, in 1913, who raised Arian to nobility. His marriage to an English baroness, Lady Meredith Norton, had been prearranged and took place shortly after his royal ceremony. They lived together in Darlington Palace until the viscount died of depression in 1920.

They had a daughter called Grace and a little boy, George, who they named after the King. Rumour had it, when the war had finished, Arian decided to make up the time he couldn't spend with his children and abandoned his noble duties. He decided to stay within the four walls of his palace on most days and played with his children. Even though they got paid, nannies were hardly ever asked to look after them. Some people believed these nannies to be the sources of the rumours surfacing around the affairs of the family.

The viscountess was said to have been a cold and ambitious lady. She only ever saw her children at teatime. The viscount, however, had a warm and friendly personality. He watched his children play all day and every night, without fail, he paid them a visit before they went to bed to kiss them goodnight. The viscountess used to make fun of him. 'Real gentlemen don't do that,' she would say to him every time.

In the summer of 1919, at the age of two, little George died of the Spanish flu. A tragedy from which the viscount could never heal. He was taken by depression a few months after. The pain of missing him, for his heart, was just too much to feel.

As Beatrice kept reading the entries of the life of Arian, who she, only a few weeks ago, thought to have been her true love and a friend, she began to understand the reasons for her imaginings. All her life she was looking for her Prince Charming and she never noticed anyone's attention unless they dressed or talked appropriately. Now she started to realise that what people deemed appropriate was not always what made them happy. These lords and ladies, living in abundance and in possessions of grand and beautiful things, but never allowed to show their true feelings, had not always been carefree.

Arian was a hostage.

His sadness was only ever released in his communications with his best friend, Teddy. They were childhood friends, but after Arian's marriage, they hardly ever met. Teddy was of no rank whatsoever and Arian felt he could be himself around him without having to worry about tradition and etiquette. Teddy was reported among the dead in the Battle of Albert at the end of the summer in 1918. Another loss that had a huge effect on the viscount's happiness.

My dear friend, Teddy,

Today I had a journey on memory lane. I remembered when we were children. I remembered you, butt naked, jumping into the lake. I can still hear the girls laughing from a distance. It wasn't very gentlemanlike, but it was funny in that instance. Don't you just miss that? Not being watched, judged? I miss the times terribly when we could do anything we wanted. A little less has changed for you, I guess, but my good behaviour is always demanded. I can't wait until we meet again.

After the war, class and all that will hopefully disappear. And, who knows, we might even jump in the lake again.

> *Your affectionate friend,*
> *Arian*
> *(August 27th, 1918)*

Dear Arian,
We thank you so much for your kindness in thinking of our son. Your letter to Edward arrived safe. We regret to say that we were told by the British Red Cross that Edward was shot dead in the Battle of Albert in August, on the 23rd day. We appreciate that you will share our loss as a great personal sorrow. Not a single moment goes by that we do not think of him, and we will cherish his joyous personality in our memories forever.

> *With our heartfelt sympathies,*
> *The McManus family*
> *(September 23rd, 1918)*

My dear friend, Teddy,
Today we buried our darling George. The ceremony could not have been grander. It was a beautiful day. Please take good care of him. You must promise me that you will. I hope it won't be long until we meet again. My days without you and my little boy are rainy and grey. Meredith and I hardly ever speak, and it is for the best, we both believe. I sit in my drawing room most days, writing my letters to you. I only share my sorrows for our darling Grace. I hear she enjoys the company of our nannies. She doesn't need me anymore. I sure miss

our times together and I miss your laughter. I wish you were here and helped me make this terrible pain go away. Do take care of yourself and my darling boy. Until we meet again.

> *Your affectionate friend,*
> *Arian*
> *(July 17th, 1919)*

Lady Meredith Froberville became one of the most talked about ladies in the county due to her tragedies. Because she never remarried, most people had compassion for her. There were, however, the few that believed her to be using her tragedies heartlessly for her ambitions.

When her daughter, Grace, grew up, she became the trustee of most local charities. She had compassion for war widows, and for the families who lost their loved ones during the flu, she shared her greatest sympathies. She was seen to be present at local events, supporting these causes, and she was celebrated by many. She was kind, she was thoughtful, and full of generosity.

'I would never have doubted that,' said Beatrice with a smile. She looked up from the book she was reading, and she realised she was the only person left in the building. With not having anything to eat since breakfast, by now, Beatrice was starving. She had several missed calls and a few messages left on her phone. All of them wondering about her well-being. She closed the book, tidied up around her, and thanked the receptionist.

Standing outside the front door, she took a deep breath. Still feeling like she just awoke from a dream, she looked around the square to see if there was a shop anywhere near. It was only then that she spotted the memorial in the middle. She crossed the road, walked close enough to read the names, and there it was.

"Edward William McManus". With tears falling down her cheeks, frozen to the ground, Beatrice stood.

Chapter 23

'I know it feels like a barrier, but we do need to make sure people feel safe when they're at the hotel.' Beatrice heard Nita briefing the team as she entered the building. She was thrilled to be back at work and even though a lot had changed, she was happy again. There were no gala dinners, in fact, they couldn't take bookings larger than fifteen. Even those were only allowed if they were to do with someone's wedding. Guests, however, started to check into the hotel. Either for pleasure or business, that didn't matter. It was ever so uplifting to see everyone together. Visors had to be worn by all and guests had to use a one-way system, following signs stuck onto the floor.

'Our lives at the hotel, as we knew it, will never be the same again. Don't forget, we are being watched, we need to refrain from group chatting.' Nita was encouraging, and clear. 'Make sure you clock out, and then you're free to leave. Hey, how are you feeling?' she asked as she walked up to Beatrice.

'I'm good. I heard how well you handled all of this.'

'We do have a good team, Beatrice. It was a smooth opening.'

'I'm immensely proud of you, Anita, you are ready to be promoted.'

'Thank you, Beatrice, but I doubt it. Let's get you updated before we get all excited.'

'I'm serious. I've been asked to join the team in head office. For my position, I'm going to recommend they take you on.'

'Wow, seriously? I can't believe what you're saying.' Nita was pleased, unable to hide it.

'You deserve it,' said Beatrice. 'Unfortunately, there can be no hugging.'

Beatrice walked towards the drawing room. Before she went inside, she looked around to make sure there was nobody by her side. The room was clean, and it gave her a loving feeling. She walked up to the fireplace. Above it, there was a portrait hanging. She never stopped to look at it before. It was a painting of a gentleman, and a little boy. The little boy was smiling. Beatrice remembered the night when, in that same room, she saw Arian's little boy the first time. She remembered he was singing. And this time, she was able to recall the lyrics.

"I had a little bird.

Its name was Enza.

I opened the window.

And in-flu-enza."

As she stood there in silence, everything started to make sense to her. Arian saved her from depression, of that, Beatrice was sure. He told her what not to do and how not to feel alone. Everything he was going through a hundred years ago. Beatrice remembered how the drawing room used to make her feel. It was dark and cold but, to her, ever so dear. She remembered New Year's Eve. In the gardens, with Arian, unhappy and wretched. No wonder he looked so sad. His life was dictated to him. By others, pre-planned. All of a sudden, Beatrice was happy to be free. Gentleman or not, she couldn't be with somebody whose love for her she didn't feel. From that moment, she had a different view on life. She had beautiful family and friends, and she believed love would come in its own time.

As she closed the door, she felt relieved. About her new job, she was thrilled. What excited her more, however, was the time she decided to spend with other people. She took Mrs Bonington out to lunch every month. She decided to see her family more often than not. She wasn't going to let life run by her anymore. She couldn't wait to go on holidays; she wanted to travel, she wanted to explore.

She had a newly found desire to organise charity events. It was the most rewarding feeling Beatrice ever felt. She did a Google search and she volunteered to help raise funds for different organisations. Among them, she became trustee of the Grace Froberville Foundation. It was her favourite. They cared the most about education and children.

***

'And they accepted you, just like that?' asked Nick.

They were sitting in Beatrice's garden. It was the middle of September, and they decided to make the most of what was left of the summer.

'Well, I volunteered. I presented a good case, I believe.'

'We're happy for you,' said Frances.

'I can't believe you have three children. Such a beautiful family. I've never been this happy,' said Beatrice.

'A lot has happened this year, but we all learned from it. So, let's celebrate.' Marilena opened a bottle of champagne.

'Thank you for looking after Beatrice,' said Nick. They hadn't met since.

'Not at all. What's more important, however, is that we're getting through it. Everyone together.'

Beatrice spent the afternoon in the company of her best friends and family. She was watching everybody laughing. It was a wonderful feeling. The world was becoming more forgiving. She didn't understand why she was so desperate before. She had the most loving family and friends, and that's more than she could ever

LOVED BY A GENTLEMAN

ask for. It was an exuberating feeling. She played with the children for the rest of the evening.

* * *

'Thank you all for coming, and here's to a successful boutique.'

Marilena's launch party was simply wonderful. The whole place looked incredible. How she managed to put her fabulous taste into every detail, to Beatrice, was unbelievable.

'Congratulations, Miss Marilena, I only have one question. Can you tell me what Logan's doing here?'

'What do you mean? He's my friend, I had to invite him.'

'You were only allowed to invite five people, miss. Is that how close you are to him?'

'Just go over there and speak to him. He's ever so charming.'

Marilena was right, Beatrice couldn't deny. Logan was handsome and he had devotion in his eyes. In that instance, he was looking at Beatrice from a distance.

Beatrice walked down from the gallery where she sat with Miss Marilena privately.

'Hi. I'm glad you could make it.'

Lightning Source UK Ltd.
Milton Keynes UK
UKHW020011281221
396266UK00006B/20/J